I0451306

JAMIE'S TRIALS

RAWLINS Book 3

DEBORAH WALLACE

Jamie's Trials: Rawlins Book 3

Published by Deborah Wallace

Copyright © 2019 by Deborah Wallace
4/22

ISBN 978-1-951457-03-7

Cover Art by Raymond and Deborah Wallace
Rawlins town by Raymond Wallace

All rights reserved.

This book is a work of fiction. All names, characters, places and incidents are either the product of the author's imagination or are used fictitiously. Any resemblance to actual persons, events or places is coincidental. No part of this book may be reproduced in any form by electronic or mechanical means, including information storage and retrieval systems, without written permission from the author, except for the use of brief quotations in a book review.

Chapter 1

Theron Jarvis sat at a table in the small on campus café, laptop in front of him. He'd received his summer job acceptance, and planned on setting up a new schedule for his Taekwondo Little Dragons class, but couldn't concentrate.

Jamie Ballard was leaving tomorrow morning. She'd finished school, and he still had another year of his masters program. There had to be a way he could see her regularly.

He took a gulp of coffee, now growing cold. Three years in the friend zone was enough. Two or three times a week they did friend things while he fell deeper in love with her, afraid she'd stop hanging out with him if he told her how he felt. It ended when they met for drinks. He'd tell her how he felt and hope she'd give them a chance. He'd spent a sleepless night coming up with the best way to reveal what was in his heart without scaring her away. He still hadn't decided if he'd tell her this evening that he loved her or ease into it over the summer.

"...Rawlins. What's the street address?"

The name of Jamie's hometown jolted him, forcing his attention to the men at a neighboring table. A dark haired man spoke on a phone, as he scribbled on a napkin.

Theron had never seen the two men on campus before, but Boston University was huge. The jeans and t-shirts the

1

men wore didn't help them fit in. A sinister vibe emanated from them. They didn't belong here.

"It'll be tougher taking her near home, but we'll get it done." The dark haired man tucked his phone in his pocket, and hunched over the table, wrapping both hands around his cup.

Theron kept his head tipped, as if looking at his laptop screen, but his eyes returned repeatedly to the two men.

The thinner man with curly, lighter hair glanced around. Theron typed gibberish on his keyboard.

"Where's this Rawlins place?" curly asked.

Dark hair pulled his phone back out of his pocket. "Let's see." He clicked and scrolled. "It's near Amherst."

The corners of curly's lips turned down. "If we'd done it my way, we would have had her two days ago, but now we have to snatch her where her family can protect her."

"It had to look like Jamie disappeared on her way home from school. We couldn't raise an alarm on campus. It's not his fault she left early." The dark haired man seemed to be the leader.

Theron's whole body chilled. It *was* Jamie they planned on kidnapping. Thank God she'd left early and these guys hadn't found her.

"So, we go to Rawlins." Dark hair smirked. "No one will find her in time anyway. I bet inside a couple weeks—" he lowered his voice and Theron strained to hear. "—have a strong enough spell cast that she'll do anything I tell her to."

A spell. He couldn't turn this over to the police. They'd be in over their heads. Yeah, like he wasn't. Sometimes he suspected there was more to Jamie than she let on, but this clinched it.

Curly hair leaned closer. "We don't have to rush. We can find the right time to take her. The boss doesn't need her for that big power thing until the end of July."

"Oh, we'll have her early. I'm going to have so much fun toying with her until we turn her over."

Theron pushed down his rage. He had no idea why they wanted Jamie, but he wouldn't let them get their hands on her. He could take on these two, but their boss would send others after her.

Curly squeezed his cup and the top popped off. "He'll kill you if you touch this one. You saw how he talked about her."

Dark hair chuckled. "Oh, I know I can't touch her that way, but that leaves a whole lot of other ways to have fun."

Theron shook with anger. Who were these men? What ultimate plans did their boss have for Jamie? He needed to make sure she really had left campus, then find her. But he couldn't leave before these men because they might realize he'd heard. It was the hardest thing he'd ever done, sit, and listen as the dark guy discussed how he'd torture Jamie for his own pleasure.

Theron waited only a half minute after the men left before he closed his laptop and raced out the door. He'd hoped to follow them, and maybe get a license plate number, but they were nowhere in sight.

He tore across campus and up the stairs of Jamie's dorm. Tracey caught his arm as he tried to run past. Her blonde streaked hair was cut short like a cap. She wore cut-off jean shorts with ragged edges, and a faded t-shirt. "Wait, Theron. She's not there."

He stopped. "Where is she?"

Her blue eyes sparkled, as she stared up from her five-foot height. "She left early. Her brother's getting married."

"She didn't tell me that."

Tracey laughed. "Yeah. You should have seen her. She didn't even know Jason had a girlfriend and suddenly they're getting married. She grumbled the whole time she tossed her stuff into bags and boxes after the call."

He was grateful she'd left already, even if he didn't get to see her. "Thanks, Tracey."

She touched his arm. "Give her a call."

He'd had that look from Tracey a number of times. She'd encouraged him to tell Jamie how he felt, but he'd always preferred her friendship to not having her in his life at all. "I will." She headed out the door and he pulled out his phone, to find a voicemail from Jamie. His phone had been in his locker at the dojo. He'd forgotten to check for messages after teaching the Little Dragons class.

"Hi, Theron. Mom called and told me Jason is getting married this weekend. Can you believe it? I'm sorry we can't meet up for a drink tonight, but I have to leave as soon as I get everything packed up. I'll talk to you later."

He pushed the number to call her. It rang four times and went to voicemail. He hoped it was because she was still on the road, and didn't hear it ring in her purse. "Jamie. It's Theron. I overheard two guys talking about kidnapping you. Go straight home. Don't stop. I'll see you as soon as I can get there."

No way would he let anything happen to the woman he loved.

Theron ran back to the café where he'd left his car and drove to his apartment. He packed a large bag, figuring he'd be in Rawlins for quite a while. Back in the car, he gassed up and got on the road.

In the morning, he'd notify *Gleason Industries* he wouldn't be able to interning with them this summer.

The two hour drive to Rawlins should put him there about ten o'clock. The only problem was he didn't know Jamie's address, but he should be able to reach her and ask for it when he got close.

Five miles past the Auburn exit, his left rear tire blew out. He gripped the wheel and lightly tapped the brakes. The rear

4

of the car fishtailed and he worked to keep it in his lane. A quick check of the mirrors found the right lane empty, so he eased over, and hit the flashers button. He crossed the rumble strip and came to a stop as far from the travel lanes as he could.

He'd never had a flat tire before, and now he'd gotten one at the worst possible time. He grabbed a flashlight from the glove box, the one his mother had given him a couple years ago for Christmas with emergency flashers on it.

He opened his trunk and shuffled the few things inside to gain access to the cover over the spare tire. He folded it back and wrenched the tire out, dropping it on the asphalt. It didn't bounce as he expected. He pushed down on it. It was flat, too.

"No!" His scream was absorbed into the woods.

He'd bought the car used a couple years ago and had never thought to check the spare tire.

Jamie's life might depend on him and he was stuck on the side of the road.

He leaned against the corner of the car, being careful not to block the flasher, as he scrolled through his phone. At least, being on the turnpike, he had good reception. Now, he had to figure out who he should call.

Blue flashing light in the distance caught his eye. Great. Well, maybe this time it would be helpful. He'd been pulled over once for speeding and gotten a warning, so state troopers weren't all bad.

Theron didn't move as the police car stopped behind his and the trooper got out.

The man touched his gun. "Got a problem there?"

"Yeah. Two flat tires. I was just trying to figure out who to call."

The trooper glanced at the tire on the ground, the one still on his car and back to Theron. "I'll call it in for you. Should have a tow truck here shortly."

"Thanks."

The cop got back in his car. Theron couldn't catch the muffled exchange.

The trooper came up to him again. "He's on another call, so it'll be about an hour before he gets here."

Theron dropped his shoulders. He couldn't protect Jamie if he wasn't with her. "Okay. Thanks."

The trooper drove away as Theron stuck the spare tire back into his trunk. He tried calling Jamie again and got voicemail. He didn't need to leave another message.

An hour and ten minutes of playing games on his phone had gotten Theron frustrated at the lost time. A flatbed wrecker pulled in front of him in the breakdown lane and backed up to his car.

A man jumped out of the cab and Theron met him halfway between the vehicles. "I hear you have a problem."

"Yeah, two flat tires."

"Sorry, man, but it's not going to go away anytime soon."

Theron sucked in a breath. "What does that mean?"

The man, the patch on his shirt said Rick, pushed a lever and the bed started to angle down in back. "The stations are closed. The best I can do is take you to one that's close to a motel. We'll leave your car there and I'll drop you at the motel. It'll be about a half mile walk in the morning."

Theron ran his hands into his hair and pulled. Could it get any worse? Don't even think that because it probably could.

Rick hooked a cable to Theron's car, dropped the car into neutral and winched it onto the truck bed, then secured it. Within fifteen minutes, they were on the road, headed to the nearest exit.

Rick glanced at Theron. "On your way home?"

"No. Visiting a girl." He couldn't very well tell the guy he planned on protecting her from some kind of evil spell.

"Tough break."

"Yeah."

After dropping the car, he checked into a motel, and tried one last time to reach Jamie. The phone rang a few times and went to voicemail. He drifted off to sleep hoping Jamie hadn't already been kidnapped.

Chapter 2

Jamie sighed as she watched Jason kiss his bride again. Since they'd rushed the wedding, the ceremony had been held at home in the library. Other than Jamie, her brother and sister and parents, the only other guests present were Shauna's best friend, Kristy, and Kristy's father, Jack Collins.

The last time she'd talked to Jason, they'd discussed their joint inheritance and his plan to use part of his share to buy a house. There'd been no mention of a fiancée. Now he glowed with love, kind of like how Dad still looked at Mom. She hoped to find someone who loved her that much.

Jamie marched up to Jason and Shauna. "Jason, I'm stealing your bride. You two are leaving tomorrow and this is the only chance I'll have to get to know my new sister-in-law."

"We'll be back in two weeks."

"Exactly. You get her for two weeks all to yourself, so you can let me have her for a little bit."

Husband and wife exchanged worried expressions.

She frowned. "Hey, you two can't do the talk-in-the-head thing like Mom and Dad, can you?"

Shauna chuckled. "No, but it sure would have made it easier to figure Jason out. Do you want to sit in those cozy chairs in the corner?" She pointed to the far side of the library.

Jamie had spent hours upon hours in that corner or on the nearby window seat, reading. Most of the old dusty books on the shelves were boring old garbage, but there were many treasures. "Perfect. Thanks, Shauna."

They sat in cushioned chairs turned at a ninety-degree angle to each other, and she inspected her brother's wife. Shauna's hair was dark and rich, some of it coming over her right shoulder. Her golden brown eyes narrowed at the coming conversation. She could see why Jason had been drawn to her, and hoped the short time they'd known each other had revealed the true Shauna to him.

Jamie started with the most important question. "What are your abilities?"

Shauna's eyebrows popped up. "What? You're a direct one. I thought people didn't talk about this stuff."

"We're family now and Mom said you're related to one of the originals, so I know you've got something." She didn't want to think about the original founder she'd descended from.

"You tell me one, then I'll tell you one."

That was probably fair. "I can make lightning."

"Jason can do that, too."

Jamie nodded and waited.

"I can levitate."

Jamie smiled. "That's cool. I don't know anyone else who can do that. What do you use it for?"

Shauna glanced down to the other end of the room. "I unload the dishwasher that way. And your brother's not the neatest man when he's, um, got something else on his mind." Her face turned pink. "So I levitate our—his—clothes and send them to the laundry room."

Jamie chuckled at the dead giveaway of why *their* clothes

9

were all over. "I can warm things with my hands."

Shauna leaned forward. "You mean, like if your coffee gets cold, you can warm it up again?"

Jamie grinned. "Yeah. That's pretty much all I do with it. In my dorm, I used to heat up my leftovers, so I didn't have to take them to the kitchen. When I first got the ability, I accidentally gave Jason a third degree burn on his arm."

"That's what that scar is. I thought he'd gotten it when he was in that paramilitary group."

Jamie tapped her knee. "Your turn."

"I can make protective bubbles around things or people." Shauna looked away and bit her lip. She seemed uncomfortable with that skill.

Jamie couldn't figure how a protective ability would bother Shauna. Maybe she'd ask Jason about it later.

"Mom can do that, too. Okay. I'm done grilling you. Well, maybe not. How did you and Jason meet? It wasn't that long ago I talked to him and he didn't mention you."

"My friend's dad hired him to protect me from my ex-fiancé. I'd overheard him talking to another guy about disposing of someone."

"Oh, wow. Kind of like *The Bodyguard* with a happier ending."

Shauna chuckled. "Way more complicated than *The Bodyguard*. It got intense a couple of times. Even Jason needed a bodyguard. Next ability?"

"I think that's enough." Shauna didn't need to know what else Jamie could do. Nobody knew. She wished she didn't know. "Welcome to the family." She got up and leaned over Shauna, giving her an awkward hug. "I'm looking forward to getting to know you better after you two get back."

***

A feather soft kiss brushed Jamie's lips. She smiled and without opening her eyes, pulled him on top of her. No clothing separated them. His hand covered her breast and squeezed lightly. Her breath stopped before it quickened. She ran a hand down his back, and when she reached his firm butt, she clasped it, eliciting a moan from him and a deepening of their kiss.

She couldn't remember when she'd felt this strong of a need. Her high school boyfriend had become a distant memory. Their lovemaking had been clumsy and not totally satisfying, but she could already tell this would be so much more.

His thigh slipped between hers and she moved closer. Better, but she wanted more. His hand moved from her breast, and she tried to protest until it slid between them and found her folds. His touch sent shivers through her. She raked her nails up his back.

He feathered kisses along her jaw. "Jamie."

She loved how her name sounded on his lips.

Just when she thought she'd explode, he moved his other leg between hers. He nudged against her opening. She wrapped a leg around his thigh, urging him. She couldn't catch her breath. The fullness as he inched in overwhelmed her.

"Are you okay?" It must have taken a lot for him to hold so still.

She nodded. "I need you to…keep moving."

He slowly slipped almost all the way out and plunged back in. She wrapped her other leg around him, and when he withdrew the next time, she pulled him back in. Over and over he filled her, as his chest skimmed her breasts and his mouth plundered hers.

Even as the pleasure and tension rose, it wasn't enough. "More." She startled when his hand slipped down her belly and found her center. With his mouth on hers, she screamed. For the first time in her life, she exploded. And he came with her.

His weight dropped onto her for a second before he turned them on their sides and covered her face in kisses, as his hand ran up and down her back.

Her breathing seemed to take forever to slow.

His voice, so familiar. "I—"

She opened her eyes to stare into…

***

Jamie jackknifed up in bed on a gasp. Theron! She'd done all that in a dream with Theron. He'd always been her best friend, nothing more. Why would she have such a dream? And it seemed more than a dream. It felt real, as if she'd see him if she turned her head. She pressed her legs together, still feeling the tingle of him inside her.

She'd never experienced a dream like that or that kind of sex. And Theron. A look at his face—or body—would bring back those memories, um, dreams. Their friendship might be threatened because she ached to run her hands all over him. She had to get this sudden lust for him under control before seeing him again.

There'd been no time to make plans, but it would probably be at least a month before she saw him. Hopefully, long enough to forget this dream ever happened.

She groaned and threw an arm over her eyes, craving Theron in a way she never had before. The friend mindset had to be firmly in place before seeing him again.

She climbed out of bed and hit the bathroom. Steam floated in the air and covered the mirror. An eye level patch had been cleared and started to mist over again. Tony had been up a while already. Her brother always had weekend plans.

Once ready to face the day, she grabbed her phone and found she'd forgotten to charge it. She plugged it into the charger on her dresser, and went down to the kitchen.

"Morning, Mom. Where is everybody?"

A few crumbs littered her mom's plate, meaning the cup of coffee she stirred would be her second. "Hi, honey. Your dad is showing a house, Tony went to a game with his friends, and I haven't seen Abby yet."

Maybe she and Abby could do something together later. Jamie dropped bread into the toaster and poured juice.

She stared at the toaster. It was nice to be home and not have to worry about the next paper to write, or the next assignment to turn in, or next class to take. Now she needed to figure out what kind of job she wanted.

The toast popped and Jamie buttered it. She turned as Abby flew into the room.

"I can't believe I overslept. I'm meeting Angie at the mall." She swiped a piece of toast from Jamie's plate and ran back out. The front door slammed in her wake.

Jamie stared at her plate. "I think a tornado came through."

Her mother chuckled. "She mentioned it yesterday, but with the wedding, it slipped my mind. Otherwise, I would have woke her."

Jamie stuck another piece of bread in the toaster and took a bite of the one from her plate. She shrugged. "Maybe we'll do something after she gets out of school tomorrow."

Jamie finished eating. "I think I'm going to read in the library for a while."

She picked out one of her mother's paperbacks about alien hunks and settled onto the couch in front of a cold fireplace. If she had her mom's ability, she could wave her hand and have a toasty fire burning.

A short time later, the front door opened and closed, and voices distracted her from the book. She dropped it and hurried to the foyer. Her mom hugged Jason's new wife.

Jamie rushed to Jason's side. "Shauna, do you mind if I steal my brother for a few minutes?"

Shauna waved. "Go ahead. I wanted to talk to Kathleen anyway."

Jamie grabbed Jason's arm and spun him around, heading back outside.

He leaned against a pillar, folded his arms and smirked.

"Don't look at me like that. Like you know something you shouldn't."

His smile widened. "You mean, like when you tried to sneak in after having sex for the first time with Luke?"

She smacked his shoulder. "You don't have to bring that up."

"Hey. I never told Dad. And I let you cry on my shoulder."

"Stop." Maybe she shouldn't try to talk to him about this, but they'd shared so much in the past. She turned away and took a step.

He grabbed her arm and turned her back. His smile had disappeared. "All right. I'm sorry. What did you want to talk about?"

Jamie took a deep breath and let it out slowly. "I had a really, real dream last night."

That smile returned. "Was there a guy in it?"

Her face grew warm and she looked down at her clasped hands.

At the sound of keys jangling, she glanced up.

He held a key out to her. "Here. Tell Mom and Dad you're going to housesit for us."

Tentatively, she took it. "What's this got to do with my dream?"

"When that guy shows up, you don't want to stay *here* with him. Been there, done that." He grimaced, and she smothered a laugh. "By the way, do you know him?"

Jason seemed to know something, and it made her nervous. She didn't want the dream to mean anything. "Of course, I know him. Do you think I'd have sex with a stranger?" She slapped her hand over her mouth.

He laughed and his eyes twinkled. He was having way too much fun at her expense. "Who is he?"

She mumbled. "Theron."

He nodded. "I like him. You did good."

"What do you mean with that?" He'd met Theron three times when he came to campus to visit her. They'd eaten out, and one time had watched some game at Theron's place. The other times, they'd stayed up half the night talking. He probably did have a good idea about Theron, but they were still only friends.

Jason squeezed her shoulder. "You'll figure it out." He took a few steps, then turned back. "Oh, you need to buy some groceries, and there's a spare key in the cabinet beside the plates. I'll text you the code for the security system."

He left her staring after him, the warm key in her palm. One thing she liked about coming home was getting the chance to see her family. If she moved to Jason's house for two weeks, she wouldn't see them as much. She slipped the key in her pocket to decide later.

***

Theron stretched and climbed out of bed. Between the motel and probably a new tire, his finances would be stretched. And he had to call *Gleason Industries* to let them know he wouldn't be working for them this summer. He'd have to cancel his classes at the Taekwondo studio. He'd miss the little kids. It didn't matter if he was broke because keeping Jamie safe was more important.

After a quick shower, he headed to the lobby with the small plastic bag that he's stuffed some clothes into. He hadn't wanted to carry his big bag back to the car.

To the left of the lobby, a housekeeper bustled as she set out muffins and checked supplies. Since it was still early, no other guests were in the dining area. He gobbled a cinnamon-apple muffin and poured a cup of orange juice, gulping half of it down before picking up a banana. He dropped his room key on the desk and headed to the door. A trash receptacle sat where the walk met the parking lot. Theron finished off the juice and dropped his cup into it, then peeled the banana and continued out to the road.

Within ten minutes, he reached the service station and entered the customer area.

A man stood at a high desk and looked up at Theron. "What can I do for you this morning?"

Theron pointed over his shoulder. "That's my Civic out there. It has two flat tires. One of them is the spare."

The man pulled out an order form. "I noticed it when I came in. The tire on the car is shredded. You'll need a new one. Your spare might be dry rotted."

Theron's heart sunk. "Can you give me prices before you start? I need to go the economy route."

"Sure thing. Let me get your details. What's the year of your Civic?"

Theron picked the cheapest tire.

The man wrote the tire number on his sheet. "We'll check the condition of the spare before deciding what to do about that."

No other customers waited and they hadn't started working on the car that sat in one bay. Maybe this wouldn't take too long.

Theron took a seat and dialed Jamie. Still no answer. He hoped she was safely home with a dead phone battery. He didn't want to think about other reasons for her not answering his call.

He picked up an old magazine to thumb through. He was in the middle of an interesting article about Space-X, when his name was called.

He approached the desk.

The man behind the counter stared down at the invoice. "You've got a new tire on your car. The spare couldn't be repaired."

Theron's heart sunk. More money.

The man grinned. "But Jeff remembered a couple days ago, a guy bought a set of tires and one was barely worn, so he gave you that one for your spare. You're all set."

Thank God. "Thanks. I really appreciate that." Theron pulled out a credit card and handed it over. Papers signed and the receipt in his hand, he headed to his car. Barring any other problems, he should be in Rawlins within forty minutes. And had no idea where to go, unless he reached Jamie.

He made good time and rolled down Main Street. There. *Ballard Real Estate and Rentals*. He stopped on the street in front of the building and hurried inside. He'd never needed Jamie's address before. People didn't write letters anymore. They emailed.

A woman glanced up from a desk scattered with papers. "Good morning. How can I help you?"

"I'm looking for Jamie Ballard."

The woman frowned. "She's not here."

"I didn't expect her to be. I'd like to get her address." If Jamie's father had been there, he'd probably have given it out. They hadn't met before, but surely Jamie had spoke of him.

"I can't give you that information."

He ran a hand through his hair. "Can you call the house phone and let me talk to someone there or call her father to okay it?"

She studied him, and he kept a steady eye on her, trying to convey his honesty.

While watching him, she picked up the phone, glanced down long enough to dial, then resumed her inspection. "Hi, Reese. It's Sam. There's a young man here asking for Jamie's address."

She held the phone out. "He wants to talk to you."

Theron stepped closer and took it. "Thanks." He put the phone to his ear. "Hi, Mr. Ballard. This is Theron Jarvis."

"Jamie's talked of you often. Why is it you're here to visit without having her address?"

Theron squeezed the back of his neck. "It was kind of last minute. Did Jamie make it home?"

"Yes. Is there a reason why she shouldn't have?"

Theron's shoulders relaxed. She was safe as far as Ballard knew. "Just checking because I couldn't get hold of her by phone." And even if he had, he'd still be in Rawlins. He didn't want to tell Jamie's father about the possible kidnapping over the phone, and he wanted to talk to her about it first.

"All right. Let me talk to Sam."

Theron handed the phone back. "He wants to talk to you."

"Yes?" Her eyes narrowed on Theron. "Okay. Bye, Reese."

She cradled the phone. "Let me see ID."

Theron fished out his driver's license and held it for her.

She studied the card. "Okay." She pulled a sticky note off a pad and wrote down an address and handed it to him. "There you go."

He raced out the door, hoping he wasn't already too late.

Chapter 3

Another sex scene. Her mother actually read this stuff? Jamie dropped the book in her lap. Maybe she was being overly sensitive because of her dream.

The doorbell rang. Since she was the only one home, she hurried to the door and flung it open.

"Theron!" She threw her arms around him, giving him a quick hug, then backed up a step. She'd occasionally hugged him, but this time it felt different. "What are you doing here?"

He drew his eyebrows together and ran a hand through his hair. "Didn't you get my message?"

Her hand flew to her mouth. "The phone battery died and I left it in my room to charge."

"When I got to town, I stopped at your father's office and got your address. It's urgent that I talk to you."

"O-okaaay." She'd left town without telling him she needed to leave early, but couldn't think of any reason why he'd follow her. "Come into the library."

He followed behind her. "Jeez, Jamie. I knew your parents had money, but I didn't expect a mansion."

She peeked over her shoulder. "It's not a mansion. It's only got eleven rooms, plus however many on the third floor."

"The apartment I grew up in could fit in this foyer."

She stopped, running her eyes around the foyer, looking into the rooms she could see from where she stood, trying to experience it the way he did. She supposed it did seem big, but she'd always compared it to the estate next door. She'd spent her first two years there, but didn't remember the inside. Passing that house gave her the willies and she always crossed the street first. She shrugged. "Sorry. It's all I know."

She sat on the couch in front of the fireplace with her back to the arm.

Theron sat close to her, but without touching. A memory of his hand on her breast flashed into her head and she pushed the thought away.

"Okay. What's so urgent that you had to drive two hours to talk to me?"

He took her hand. It must be serious. He almost never touched her. "I was in the campus coffee shop, killing time before we met up."

"I'm sorry we didn't see each other before I left."

He waved his hand. "That doesn't matter. It's good you left early."

"Why?" This made no sense. They hadn't met up and now it was good. But he drove all this way to see her because they hadn't met up?

He blew out a breath. "I overheard two men talking about kidnapping you."

"What!" Her heart rate went from fifty to a hundred in two seconds flat. Theron had to have heard wrong. Nobody would want to kidnap her. "Who? What did they say?"

"At first, I wasn't paying attention, but I heard one of them say Rawlins, and I started listening." He described the conversation.

"But I'm not a virgin."

He frowned.

Jamie pointed a finger. "Don't you judge me."

He put his hands up. "I'm not. I'm surprised they got it wrong, and I'm wondering if it's important to what they want from you. It might be some kind of ceremony or ritual."

She hugged her knees to her chest. Her birth parents had done stuff like that. They'd murdered a bunch of girls in rituals before their coven had died in a fire. She couldn't tell him she had powers these men might want to take. "You don't seem surprised with spells and rituals, like you already knew they were…that some people think they're real."

He gave her a half smile. "We both know they're real."

He'd had hours to work it through after the overheard conversation. Or had he known before that?

She pushed out a long breath. "I wish Jason hadn't left today on his honeymoon."

Theron smiled. "Don't think I can protect you?"

He had a black belt in Taekwondo, and could probably protect her from ordinary men. But these men coming after her might not be ordinary. "Maybe. Besides, you'll have to get back to Boston for your summer job."

He shook his head. "Nope. I'm not leaving your side. I called *Gleason Industries* this morning and told them I couldn't work for them this summer."

She covered her mouth, then dropped her hand. "But you were excited about it. There was a lot you hoped to learn."

He gave her hand a squeeze. "You're more important than any job."

If they needed a virgin for whatever they were doing, she might be safe once they discovered the truth, but she wasn't too keen on how they'd find out. By then they'd be in Rawlins. Or already here.

She fished Jason's key out of her pocket. "I think I'm going to have to take Jason up on his offer."

Theron stared at her hand. "What offer is that?"

"Housesit while he's gone. That way, if those guys find me, they won't find Abby."

"Your little sister?"

"Yeah."

He squinted. "And why would they change their minds and go after Abby?"

"Because she's still a virgin and has…" She trusted Theron with her life, but it could be too much if he learned that some people had abilities.

His eyes bore into her for several seconds before he spoke. "Has what?"

She pulled her lips between her teeth. A childish reaction she couldn't resist.

"You'll tell me eventually. In the meantime, I'm going to be your house guest."

She sucked in a breath. That put her one step closer to her dream and possibly losing her best friend. She should refuse, but she had no way to protect herself.

***

Jamie didn't contradict his self-invitation, but picked up the house phone and called her mother. For a second, he thought she would ask permission for him to stay at Jason's.

"Hi, Mom. Can you give me Jason's address? I'm house sitting for him." Why wouldn't she know where her brother lived?

She bit her lip as she listened. "You know?" Her father must have told her mother that Theron was in town.

She paced. "I'm still going there, so you'll have to give me his address or I'll call Jason for it."

She pulled a pad of paper from the desk and wrote something down. "All right. We'll come back for dinner in a couple days."

She put her hand on her hip. "I've known Theron for three years. Of course I'm safe with him."

She sighed. "Yes, Mother."

She hung up the phone. "Wait here while I pack."

He'd love to follow her to see the bedroom she'd grown up in. Were there posters on the walls? Did she have mementos of special events? He'd lived in five homes growing up. All apartments, until the house his mother bought the summer before his senior year of high school. None of them had felt like home. He took a seat on the couch and crossed his ankle over his knee.

A short while later, Jamie came into the library with a suitcase in her hand. "I'm ready."

Theron took her bag and led them out the door to their cars. He followed her to her brother's house, and pulled into the paved driveway beside her car, one in front of each white door of the two car garage. They'd driven through a nice neighborhood, but nowhere near as impressive as the one her parents lived in.

Despite what Jamie said, she did grow up in a mansion. Eleven rooms on the first two floors, and she didn't know how many on the third. No place he'd lived had more than five rooms, and they were all smaller than any room he'd seen in the Ballard home. He'd feel intimidated if he didn't know Jamie, and that the size of her home wasn't important to her.

Jason's house would be more comfortable, and not as imposing. Of course, being alone with Jamie would be the best part. Maybe he'd get her to see him as more than a friend.

Colorful beds of flowers circled a few trees in the front yard, one of which was a flowering tree of some kind. More flowers lined the front of the house. Rectangular gray stone covered the two story home, giving it a solid feel. It was three or four times the size of his mother's two bedroom home.

He grabbed their bags and followed her into the house, setting them down. He spotted the door for the garage, which reminded him about Jamie's car. He held out his hand. "Give me your keys and I'll hide your car in the garage."

She dug into her purse. "I didn't even think of that. They probably do know what my car looks like."

She followed him to the garage. A red Nissan Sentra sat in the closer space. He hit one of the remote door openers, and the farther door opened, revealing Jamie's car. Theron drove it in and she hit the button to hide it.

Back in the house, Jamie squealed and spun around. "I can't believe Jason bought a house."

"Why not? He just got married."

"Yeah, but he traveled the world for years. I didn't think he'd ever settle down. And now he's moved back to Rawlins."

"I guess Shauna's special."

"*Really* special." She did that lip tuck thing again.

Jamie held something back. He needed to find out her secrets, and maybe he'd feel able to finally share his.

She hurried through a doorway. "Oh, wow. I love the kitchen. I can see Jason cooking here while Shauna sits at the counter making sure he doesn't miss any ingredients."

He watched her from the doorway. Sun streamed through French doors, brightening the natural oak cabinets and black countertops. Pub chairs sat at the island on the opposite end of a cook top. He could imagine something similar. Jamie watching him put together a meal, and once he put the food in the oven, he'd kiss her until they both needed more. He'd strip off her clothes and lift her to the counter. He blinked. They were a long way from that happening, if ever.

Jamie opened the refrigerator and cabinet doors, peeking inside. She reached into one cabinet, pulled out a key, and held it out to him. "Here."

He didn't reach for it. "What's this?"

"A key to the house."

"And your brother would be all right with me having one?"

She still had her hand extended. "He told me where to find it."

"So? It doesn't mean you should give it away."

She huffed out a breath. "He knew you were coming, so just take it."

He tentatively took it. "How did Jason know that?"

Jamie brushed past him. "Let's explore."

Another thing she wouldn't tell him. He hadn't sensed her being secretive before. Maybe it had to do with being back home.

He followed her through a dining room with glass doors overlooking the yard, a living room with a brick fireplace, family room, office and half bath. Definitely not a starter home, but furnished for comfort. It was nice Jason could afford to buy this house for his bride. If—when he and Jamie married, she'd have to wait for something this nice.

She raced up the stairs and he followed more slowly, chuckling at her exuberance. She came out of the second bedroom on the left as he reached the top of the stairs, and darted into the room across the hall, coming out beside him seconds later.

Jamie pointed to the four doors. "Each pair of bedrooms is separated by a bathroom." She indicated the last door at the end of the hall. "And that must be the master bedroom."

She hurried down the hall and threw open the last door. Theron came up behind her as she stopped in the doorway.

Jamie peeked inside. "Wow. This is really nice."

A neatly made king-size bed sat close to the door. A fireplace with a fluffy rug stood between two windows. He didn't want to imagine what Jason and his wife did on that rug, but Jamie—he could stay awake half the night thinking about soft firelight and a naked Jamie.

Beyond the bed, one door led into a bathroom, and he assumed the other was a closet.

Jamie disappeared into the bathroom. "Oh, my God. I so wish I could use this."

Theron came up behind her. She stared into a deep Jacuzzi tub.

"Why can't you?"

She glanced at him like he was crazy. "This is Jason and Shauna's bathroom. There are two others I can use."

"But no Jacuzzi?"

"No."

"I'm sure they won't mind if we—you used this." He hoped she hadn't caught his slip. Images of her glistening wet had him working at keeping his breathing steady. He wanted to fill his hands with soap and run them over her breasts. Not helping.

She glanced over her shoulder, her cheeks pink, and back to the tub. She heard it. He wasn't sure yet if that was bad or good.

He went back to the hallway and took slow, even breaths. By the time she joined him, he was under control.

Jamie stopped beside him. "I was thinking that we should have rooms across from each other. That way, we can each have our own bathroom."

He nodded, but hoped that by the time the newlyweds returned, he and Jamie would be sharing one bathroom, one bedroom, and one bed. "That makes sense. You pick out the rooms and I'll go get our bags."

Theron retrieved the bags, and stopped in front of her as she stood between the second set of doors. "These?"

She nodded. "Yes. I decided that if someone broke in

26

while we were sleeping, they'd have to search the other bedrooms first."

"Good thinking." He handed her bag over and waited for her to choose a room before entering the one across from it. He gave the room a cursory scan, dropped his bag on the bed and went across the hall. She loaded her clothes into dresser drawers.

He leaned against the doorframe and watched her move gracefully between her bag and the dresser. He'd enjoyed training her in self-defense skills, and would intensify the training. It didn't ease his mind about the men coming after her. When he told Jamie about the men who wanted to kidnap her, he'd left out the part about the one man's plan to use spells to incapacitate her. He didn't want her to panic and not defend herself. It was enough for her to know that she was in danger.

She dropped the empty bag on the floor beside the dresser.

He straightened up. "I should go shopping."

She gasped and spun around, her hand over her heart. "Theron. You scared me half to death."

"Sorry."

Jamie crossed her arms and leaned back against the dresser. "No. I'm coming. Those guys aren't likely to go to a grocery store." She tucked her long, dark hair under a baseball cap she found in the coat closet. "Let's go."

Normally, Theron found grocery shopping tedious, but he'd make sure to brush against Jamie as much as he could, figuring she'd be more comfortable close to him in public, and maybe she'd start to see him differently.

***

Shopping with Theron was fun. It almost felt like they

were a couple, figuring out what meals to make, which snacks to buy. Jamie pretty much knew what foods he liked, but he surprised her when he picked out ingredients to make chicken cordon bleu from scratch.

He laughed at her when she stared blankly at him after he picked up asparagus.

One of his eyebrows lifted. "You don't like asparagus?"

She smirked. "I love asparagus. I didn't think you would."

He tapped an asparagus spear on her nose. "You don't know everything about me."

And he knew less about her than he thought he did, too.

Up and down the aisles they went, dropping bottles, boxes and cans into the cart. Since Theron was next to it, she tossed a box of Cheerios at him, and he caught it, dropping it beside his Rice Chex.

"Hey, if I wasn't paying attention, you could have hit me with that."

She laughed. "Aren't you glad I didn't throw that can of beans?"

He laughed, picked her up at her waist and spun her around once before setting her back down. He stared into her eyes for several seconds before releasing her. She got the weirdest impression that he wanted to kiss her, but this was Theron. The closest he'd come were brotherly type kisses on the forehead or top of her head. She accepted them for what they were, but maybe she wanted a kiss that wasn't at all brotherly.

As they stood in line at check-out, she extracted her debit card from her wallet.

He reached for his wallet. "I'll pay."

She waved the card in front of his face. "No you won't. You've given up your internship to protect me. I know the money you make over the summer gets you through the school year." Along with the extra from teaching Taekwondo.

He huffed out a breath. "All right, but next time I'll pay for groceries."

At home, they put away the food, except for the chicken and asparagus.

Theron pointed to a chair. "You can sit and watch or go read."

Jamie hopped up onto the pub chair and laced her fingers on the counter. "I'll watch." He hadn't cooked for her before, and she wanted to see how good he was. And she didn't want to be away from him.

He found a meat tenderizer and flattened the chicken breasts. With the way he whacked them, she suspected he was thinking about what he wanted to do to the men searching for her. He added Swiss cheese and ham, and rolled them up, then dipped them in egg and bread crumbs, and dropped them on a baking sheet. The sheet went into the oven and Theron set the timer.

"Wow. You really seem to know what you're doing."

He broke off the ends of asparagus. "Chicken was inexpensive, so Mom used to make that for us all the time." He held up a spear. "But asparagus is expensive. We hardly ever had it."

She'd never thought of chicken cordon bleu as being inexpensive to make. Her mom had made it a few times, but more often, bought the frozen packages to pop into the oven. She'd never thought about the expense of food. Sure, she knew that she had nicer clothes than some of the other kids at school, and was gifted a newer used car when she got her driver's license, but she figured food was food. It never occurred to her that some people had to grocery shop with care.

They talked like old times, before the Theron dream. She

only got distracted a couple of times as he chopped vegetables for two small salads, remembering what else those hands could do.

During the delicious dinner, conversation stayed on light topics, never veering to the danger she was in. She didn't think about it often, but every once in a while, she wondered if the men were in Rawlins already.

A long evening stretched before them. Jamie couldn't remember how many times she and Theron had spent an evening watching TV. But this time was different. This wasn't the common room at her dorm, or the sports bar where they watched a game. There'd been times they watched a movie or game at Theron's apartment, but those times were few and far between, and only because she wanted to cook. In that way, they weren't friends like she would be with another girl. No giggling together, or sharing secrets. No sleepovers.

It was just the two of them in a house with five beds, two couches and a spa tub. Now, she could have whatever kind of sleepover she wanted. Maybe. She'd never felt this nervous around Theron before. She hoped he didn't notice the way her hands shook or see the pulse in her neck beating a fast tattoo. If not for that damn dream, everything would feel normal.

In the family room, Jamie picked up the TV remote and sat on one end of the couch, and flipped through channels. She chose a comedy that had barely started.

Theron came in carrying two glasses of wine. Usually, at a bar, Theron drank beer, so she'd been surprised when he bought a bottle of wine along with the beer. He handed her one, and she wasn't at all surprised when he took the middle cushion.

He chuckled at the show. She'd been so aware of him beside her, and trying unsuccessfully to push thoughts of that dream away, she hadn't heard one word said on the screen.

He laughed outright, then frowned at her. Normally, she'd laugh right along with him.

"Hey, are you too tired to pay attention to the show? Maybe you should hit the sack early."

She stared into his worried eyes. If only he knew. No. He wouldn't want to know. She looked away. "I'm tired. I'm worried. I know I won't sleep."

He kissed the top of her head. He'd done it hundreds of times before. It probably wasn't any different this time, but with the dream making her aware of him as a sexy man, and not just her best friend, it felt totally different.

"I saw books in the office. Why don't you pick one out, go to bed, and read until you fall asleep?" He grinned. "Just don't pick a scary one. I don't want to be awakened in the middle of the night with you screaming from a nightmare."

A perfect solution. For tonight, anyway. "That's a great idea. Thanks." She stood.

He reached out his hand. "Do you want me to take that?"

She stared into her wineglass. "No. I think I'll top it off and take it with me. Goodnight, Theron."

***

After watching Jamie leave, Theron dropped his head to the back of the couch. Something seemed different with her. She'd seemed a bit uncomfortable sitting beside him. Sometimes while they watched TV, she used to lean against him, but this time, she seemed determined to keep her distance. Maybe it was because they were alone in this house. He'd always been careful to have people around them, and rarely had her come to his studio apartment. He couldn't trust himself to stay in the friend zone.

Now he had to figure out how to make the transition to

boyfriend, but give them the out to go back to friends if that's all she wanted. That wasn't at all what he wanted anymore.

He ran his hands through his hair and joined them behind his neck. Maybe he'd offer her a massage. Neck, shoulders, back. If it seemed to turn her on, he could go a little further. Or a lot further. Like the Jacuzzi.

He let out a long breath. She had to be the one to lead or he'd spoil everything between them. He needed to provide opportunities to nudge things along.

He didn't want all or nothing. If he couldn't have it all, he'd back off to friends only. At least for a little while, until he found a different way to make Jamie fall for him.

Chapter 4

Theron woke to the smell of bacon and coffee. He threw sweats on over his briefs, and headed down the stairs, already enjoying this playing house thing. In the kitchen, disappointment flared to see Jamie already dressed.

She wasn't wearing his old shirt. A couple years before, she'd confiscated a t-shirt he'd spilled ketchup on, saying she'd use it for a nightshirt. Twice since then, he'd given her well worn t-shirts that he'd said he was done with, in order to get her to wear something of his, even if he'd never see it on her.

He came up behind her, crowding her space, and reached around her to snatch a piece of bacon off the plate she loaded with scrambled eggs. She smelled better than the bacon, the flowery soap she used and her special scent.

The salty meat tasted as good as it smelled with the perfect crunch. "Thanks for making breakfast."

"You're welcome. And that's your plate now."

He chuckled, and couldn't resist kissing the top of her head. He poured coffee into the nearby cup and topped hers off.

She held both plates, and he picked up her cup, following her to the kitchen table.

Theron bit into a piece of toast and followed it with a

swallow of coffee. "I thought I'd check out the historical society this morning."

She raised her eyebrows. "Really? You want to find out about Rawlins' past?"

"Don't look surprised. Look how many museums I've dragged you through. I'm curious. Especially since you once told me your mom's maiden name is Rawlins. Do you want to come?"

She shook her head. "No. I already know everything I want to know about Rawlins. I think I'll stay here, relax and hide my face."

"I should have thought of that staying hidden part."

She tore the crust off her toast. "Mom wants us to come to dinner tomorrow."

"Sure. I'd love to meet your family."

She blushed, and he bit his tongue to hold back a joyful laugh. She was starting to think of him as more than a friend.

"Um, okay." Her blush deepened. "Mom probably thinks we're sleeping together since we're all alone here." Her eyes remained on her food.

"It's not like we didn't have opportunities in Boston, if that's what we wanted." And he so much wanted. He wished she'd look at him, so he'd know how she reacted to that. "Talk to her privately when we get there, or you can go alone." Her discomfort was the last thing he intended.

"We are in separate bedrooms. That makes it a whole lot easier. And I've talked about you for three years. They practically know you."

Finally, he saw her eyes. She'd masked them. Whatever thoughts went through her head were now hidden. A month ago, she would have made a joke about her mother thinking they were sleeping together. Her feelings for him were in transition, and if he wasn't careful, he might lose her all together.

He stood. "I'm going to shower."

***

Once he was dressed, Theron found Jamie in the living room, reclined on the couch, a book clutched in her hands. "I'm leaving now. Stay indoors."

She waved. "I won't venture out without you."

Theron had driven past *Rawlins Historical Society* on his way through town the day before, and reached it in minutes. He'd guess that the white clapboard building had once been the town hall or meeting house. He hadn't thought to check hours, but fortunately, the wait on a bench near the door was only seven minutes.

A woman with short blonde hair and a flowing skirt ran up the steps to the door. "I'm so sorry I'm late. My cat escaped just as I was leaving and I had to catch her."

Theron jumped up. "It's fine. You're only two minutes late."

She turned the key in the lock. "I'm usually here fifteen minutes before we open to get everything organized and the lights on."

He followed her into the building. "Don't worry about it."

She flipped a light switch at the door and tapped a book. "Can you sign our guest register?"

He signed his name and filled in his city as light switches flicked on throughout the building.

The woman stopped before him. She'd tucked her purse away and put on a name badge—Ms. Mathews. "What brings you here today?"

"I'm visiting a friend and thought I'd find out more about her hometown."

"Oh. What's your friend's name?"

"Jamie Ballard."

The woman's mouth thinned. "Oh, her. It was very sad."

He frowned. "What's sad?"

"Her parents died in a fire when she was a baby."

"No. They're alive."

"The Ballards adopted Jamie and Jason. Let me show you the family tree."

He followed her into another room. She stopped in front of a large plastic coated paper on the wall. "This is the Rawlins founders' family tree." She pointed to two squares. "As you can see, Jamie and Jason were born to Nathan and Elise Proctor."

Did it mean something that Jamie had never told him about being adopted? If this woman knew, Jamie had to know. The way she talked about her family, she was close to all of them. Maybe she rarely thought about it.

He scanned the names of the founders. Ballard wasn't amongst them, but some seemed familiar. "Where did they come from?"

"They left Salem Village after the witch hysteria ended."

The name sent a jolt up his spine. "I'm from Danvers."

It didn't seem to faze her. He would think that someone who worked at the historical society would know about the connection. He stood straighter, happy to enlighten her. "Salem Village is contained in what is now Danvers."

Ms. Mathews eyes widened. "Oh. I should have known that. So, does your family go very far back in Danvers?"

"We go back to the Bradstreets." The story that was passed down through his family was that John Bradstreet had been accused of witchcraft and was going to flee with his wife, but she became too sick to travel. Fortunately, the trials ended and everyone still imprisoned were freed before he'd been arrested.

She frowned. "I'm not familiar with much of the hysteria history since that was before Rawlins' history."

36

He didn't expect to give a history lesson when he came to learn about Rawlins. "John Bradstreet was named just before it ended. I wouldn't be here if he hadn't been lucky." He glanced at the top of the family trees. "Do you have anything on these founders?"

"Yes. Which ones are you interested in?"

"Proctor and Rawlins. Where does Ballard come in?" He wondered if Jamie had visited the historical society to learn about the town's past or if there were family records.

"Actually, a Bishop daughter married a Ballard in 1860."

Nearly half the founders were connected to Jamie.

Ms. Mathews led him to a bookcase, and pulled out a one inch volume, handing it to him. "Here are biographies of all seven founders for a nice overview. Then there—" she pointed to three shelves "—are specific biographies and some of their writings. Joseph Rawlins was the most prolific, as was his daughter."

"Thank you." He sat at a table near the bookcase and opened the book. A table of contents helped him find the correct sections. About twenty pages were dedicated to each man.

Theron found that Joseph Rawlins, Kathleen Ballard's ancestor, organized the group that fled Salem Village. Although, he wasn't sure he would call it fled, since they left shortly after the witch hysteria ended. Maybe Joseph didn't like the way people mistrusted each other after that.

Edward Bishop, Reese Ballard's ancestor, didn't seem to have any history that stood out.

The most important person to Theron was John Proctor, since he was a direct ancestor by blood to Jamie. He was the son of the executed John Proctor, and married Rebecca Parris just before leaving with Joseph Rawlins. Theron could imagine John's daily pain of seeing the people who caused his father's death. He died in a barn fire with his oldest son and others. Some mystery involved how they'd been trapped.

Next, Theron pulled out papers about John Proctor. He didn't seem to have written journals like some of the other founders had. Mostly, the papers showed his land holdings, and one puzzling set of papers about a missing girl. He'd been the last person seen with her. An accusation had been made against him, but was soon dropped. It probably was nothing.

Theron pulled out his phone and checked the time. He'd been away from Jamie for three hours, and needed to get back to her. He stopped by the desk where Ms. Mathews sat and thanked her before stepping out into the sunshine.

He dialed Jamie.

"Hi, Theron." He loved the sound of her voice. It almost always had an underlying excitement, like she knew a surprise waited around every corner.

"Hi, Jamie. I'm done here. Shall I pick up take-out?"

She laughed. "Rawlins doesn't really have take-out, but you can order meals to be boxed up at your choice of two restaurants. Don't bother, though. I already have dinner in the oven."

He loved Jamie's cooking. Those were the rare times she spent at his apartment, using his kitchen. "Great! I'll be home in a few." Home. He wondered if it felt as good to Jamie to hear as it had for him to say. He pocketed his phone and hurried to his car.

***

Jamie sat in the family room, flipping channels on the TV, as she waited for Theron to clean up after dinner. Her cheeks still felt flushed from all the praise he'd given her over her simple enchilada and red rice dinner. She'd cooked meals for him before, and he'd tell her how he appreciated it, but this was over the top. There was a definite change in how he treated her, and she didn't understand it.

She clicked through channels as Theron came in, sat down beside her, and took away the remote. He turned the TV off and took her hands in his. "I found out something interesting today."

"Oh?" The couple of times she'd asked about his Rawlins research, he'd changed the subject. It had worried her that he didn't want to talk about it.

"I didn't know that Rawlins was established by people fleeing the witch hysteria."

"Yeah. They left Salem in 1693."

He shook his head. "No. They left Salem Village."

"What's the difference?"

"They were neighboring towns. Do you know where I'm from?"

Of course she knew. He'd taken her to his mother's a few times. "Danvers."

"Danvers used to be called Salem Village. Your ancestors might have known my ancestors."

Her breath caught and she squeezed his hands. Maybe some force had brought them together. It had happened with her parents. "Mom said her parents left Rawlins and then she came back when she inherited her uncle's property. She met Dad as soon as she got here and they knew they were supposed to be together."

"Wha—"

She put her hand over his mouth. "Then Jason was hired to protect Shauna and he brought her here. It turned out that her grandmother was from Rawlins. And now they're married. Mom said that Rawlins calls its own home."

Theron tipped his head. "And why are you telling me this?"

"Maybe you're supposed to be here. Maybe your

ancestors were supposed to come."

He stared at her as his chest expanded with deep breaths. "My ancestor would have been hanged, except the hysteria ended in time. Maybe if his wife hadn't been sick, he would have gone with the Rawlins group."

"You might have been born here?"

He chuckled. "I'm sure my ancestors would have married different people, so it wouldn't have been me." He sobered. "I found out something about you."

Her heart fluttered and she bit her lip. "That I'm adopted?"

He nodded. "Why didn't you ever tell me?"

"Then I'd have to tell you about those parents. I have a good life as a Ballard. I wouldn't be the same person without these parents. Jason and I don't want the Proctor name."

It was rare for her to think of her birth parents. Hate wasn't strong enough for how she felt about them and that name, but if things between her and Theron headed in the direction of the dream, he needed to know.

She looked away then at their joined hands. Maybe he wouldn't want to touch her once he heard. "My birth father, Nathan Proctor, and his wife were part of a cult and they were…" She took a breath and let it out. "Serial killers."

He released her hands and her heart ached.

He wrapped his arms around her and pulled her onto his lap. "I'm so sorry. But you're not them. You're your own person. I've known you for three years and you're the kindest person I know."

She sagged against him. She'd never been on his lap before, but right now it's what she needed. To be close to him. To know that he didn't hold her responsible for what her birth parent had done. "Thank you. I've never told anybody that. I was afraid they'd think I inherited a crazy gene."

He tightened his arms around her for a second. "No. Just

sweet Jamie." He kissed her cheek.

She liked it, liked snuggling into him, but if she stayed there much longer, it might get awkward. She lifted her head and his lips claimed hers in a gentle kiss. She pulled back a few inches and stared into his eyes. That expression had never been on his face before either. It was almost like at the end of her dream when she discovered who she'd made love with.

Slowly, he brought his face to hers again and gave her another kiss. "I—"

She put her hand over his mouth. Whatever he was going to say, she wasn't ready to hear it. "I have to go to bed now. Goodnight, Theron." She scrambled off his lap and hurried from the room.

Chapter 5

The next morning, Theron sat in the kitchen, sipping his coffee. A sense of calm flowed through him. And quiet. The niggling feeling that touched him as he drifted off to sleep blossomed. A protection spell guarded the house.

He and his mom had cast one over their house in Danvers. He'd purposely not done it on campus, not knowing if there were some who could detect it.

Since Jason and Shauna hadn't been in the house long, the previous owners could have placed it. He leaned toward Jason or Shauna doing it, which meant one or both of them had special abilities.

Jason had to have abilities. He grew up in Rawlins, a town founded by people who left Salem because of the witch trials. There was only one reason they would have left when they did. They feared the townsfolk would discover their real abilities. If the ancestors had them, then Jason likely did, and his sister, too.

He could sense Jamie's underlying strength, but never taken the time before to figure out what that meant. He'd known Jamie was different the first time he met her at a super bowl party, but never pinpointed in what way. She was more special than he'd thought.

No wonder someone hired those guys to kidnap her.

Why hadn't she told him she had abilities? He sighed. They'd grown really close and he hadn't told her what he could do either. Like him, she'd probably been trained to not tell anyone about her special abilities. It was time to give up their secrets.

Right after breakfast.

Pushing the discovery aside, he moved to the cabinets. He found ingredients and pans, then concentrated on the meal preparation. He set the table between pancake flips and turning sausage links. The gurgle of coffee dripping ended, and he poured a cup.

"That smells delicious."

He glanced at her tousled hair. The way he imagined it would look after they'd been in bed together. If only he could bury his hands in it, and pull her close for a kiss. "You look tired. Couldn't sleep?"

She stifled a yawn. "This dream of being captured by two men kept replaying through my head." She rubbed her forehead. "It was a really weird dream."

"What did these men look like?" He hoped she hadn't had a premonition.

She squinted. "There was a taller, thinner one with medium brown hair, and a long nose. The other one had shoulder length, dark hair, with a bit of a curl. And his expression was almost always a sneer."

He gripped her upper arms. "Those are the men from the café!" A premonition. Another sign that Jamie had abilities. Her dream could mean the men were in Rawlins.

She shook her head furiously, and her eyes widened. "No. It couldn't be."

"Come have breakfast. We'll talk about it after." He wanted them to have full stomachs before having the discussion he dreaded.

"Thanks."

Through the meal and clean-up, he kept her mind off her worry with small talk about school.

He took her hand. "Let's go to the family room. We have to talk." He'd touched her more in the last two days than in the last six months, and he liked it.

Without releasing her hand, he sat on the couch with her beside him. The sun threw a long light across the floor, warming the carpet in front of the couch.

Jamie's brows came down and she squinted, her hand trembled.

He hated that he had to do it this way. "We seem to be in a really safe place. Who put the protection spell on the house?"

Her mouth dropped open then she bit her lip. "H-how do you know that?"

He shrugged. "It was really quiet this morning and the feeling settled in. I can sometimes sense the use of abilities. Who did it? Jason?"

Her eyes grew wide, but she said nothing.

"Come on, Jamie. It's me. You know I wouldn't do anything to hurt you. I came here to help."

She let out a long breath and her shoulders slumped. "You sensed it?" Her eyes locked on his for long seconds. "It was probably Mom and Dad. They repeat the spell at our house four times a year."

"Good. At least you'll be partially safe at either house."

She sat straighter, pushing her shoulders back. "How do you know about protection spells?"

"I have one on my mother's house."

She tugged her hand from his and covered her mouth. The loss nearly gutted him. "You have abilities?"

He noticed how she didn't call them powers, or ask if he was a warlock. "Yes. What are yours?"

She pulled her lips in, then burst out. "You first."

44

"Okay. I can push things."

She squinted. "What does that mean?"

He concentrated on a pillow on the end of the couch and threw it across the room.

She giggled. "That's helpful. In a pillow fight."

"It's also helpful if I'm jumped. It's like two of me fighting."

Her eyes widened. "Has that happened?"

"A couple of times. I can handle myself. That's one reason I want to be here to protect you. I can also sense when someone uses their abilities. There's residual power. That's how I knew about the protection spell on the house. I would have noticed right away if they'd done it yesterday. Now you."

"I can warm things with my hands. Pretty much only useful for keeping my coffee hot."

"No. Don't discount it. That's a good self-defense skill. If someone tries to kidnap you, you can burn him. What else?"

"I can make lightning, but I don't see how I can use that. If someone grabs me, I'd electrocute myself, too."

He rubbed his chin. "Yeah. I guess…you could use it if you saw them coming and they weren't close yet."

"But if they aren't close yet, I won't know if they mean me harm, and I don't want to possibly kill an innocent."

His voice hardened. "Well, don't get any qualms if you see those men from that premonition. How did you find out you could create lightning?" Most abilities were inherited, and Jamie's adopted parents probably didn't know what her birth parents could do.

She blushed and stared at her lap. There was definitely a story there.

Theron tucked a finger under her chin and lifted. "What happened?"

Her eyes met his. "It happened"—her eyes closed and she

drew in a breath—"The first time I had sex."

Okay. Not at all what he expected. He hadn't planned on talking about past sexual experiences with her. "Um. Does it happen every time you have sex?"

Her eyes widened. "No!"

His shoulders relaxed. If his plans worked out, he and Jamie would be having sex. A lot. He didn't want freak lightning storms every time. "How did you know it was you?"

Her eyes didn't meet his again. "After we, um, started, power gradually increased inside me. Then it left in a rush when lightning cracked nearby. So close, it set off my boyfriend's car alarm."

He laughed, imagining some boy scrambling for his key fob when he still wanted to be doing his girl. And he wasn't going to think about that being Jamie.

Long minutes passed where all he heard was Jamie's breathing slowing to normal.

Her voice was hesitant. "What else can you do?"

"Sorry, baby. That's it for me." The endearment slipped out, and he wondered if she noticed. He should be mending their friendship, not forging ahead. He took a chance and glanced at her. "What about you?"

She looked away, and bit her lip. "That's it."

He didn't believe her. There was more she could do, but didn't want to tell him. He wondered if it was something she was embarrassed by or worried about. He wouldn't push her now. "Since your parents have abilities, I think we should tell them about this threat. They'll probably understand it and can help protect you."

"I hate to worry them."

He rested his hand on her shoulder and massaged it. "I know, but they'd skin me alive if something happened to you and we didn't let them help."

She smiled. "You're probably right. I'll give Mom a call and tell her I'm bringing you to dinner."

He hoped they didn't accuse him of playing house with their daughter, and order him to leave. It wasn't happening. He would refuse to leave.

***

Family dinner seemed to take forever. Jamie hated pretending nothing was wrong as she caught up with her parents, Tony sat at the table, but Abby had dinner with a friend so they could work on a school project.

Jamie had talked about Theron often, but he'd only met Jason at school, and never the rest of her family. Being a friend and not her boyfriend, there'd never been a reason to bring him home on a long weekend, although she had met his mother.

Theron handed her plates and she placed them in the dishwasher. One step closer to that conversation she dreaded.

"Theron, do you want to play a video game?" her brother asked.

"Another time, Tony. Jamie and I have to talk to your parents."

Tony lowered his voice. "She's not pregnant, is she?"

Jamie gasped. "Tony, that's not even funny."

Tony lifted an eyebrow. "I wasn't trying to be funny. Does that mean no?"

Theron gripped Tony's shoulder. "It's something else we have to talk about." He spun Tony around and gently pushed him out of the kitchen.

She took deep breaths, hoping it might help her flaming face return to normal. They hadn't had sex. Why did that question affect her so badly? Probably that crazy Theron dream. And then she wondered what it would feel like to

47

have Theron's baby growing inside her. Those deep breaths she'd tried for were gone, replaced with quick puffs that did nothing to oxygenate her brain.

Theron put his hands on her shoulders with his face inches from hers. "Jamie, are you okay? Are you having a panic attack?"

He steered her to the kitchen table and pushed her into a chair. She crossed her arms on the table and dropped her head onto them. Jeez. She'd so overreacted to Tony's tactless question.

Theron crouched beside her, his hand petting her head. "Jamie?"

"I'm still here," she rasped.

He chuckled, and massaged her neck. "That you are. We don't have to talk to your parents tonight, if you don't want to."

She took a couple of deep breaths and lifted her head, not looking at him. "No. We should talk to them ASAP." She wondered if he had any idea what had gone through her head. She stood and marched to the door and into the library.

Kathleen and Reese sat on the couch in front of a gentle fire in the fireplace. After Theron entered, she closed the pocket doors.

Both parents' heads shot up.

"We have to talk to you."

Her parents glanced at each other.

"And no talking in your heads to each other."

Kathleen's eyes widened and went to Theron before settling on her daughter. "Jamie!"

Jamie sat in the chair kitty corner to the couch and Theron sat on the arm beside her. "Theron knows about abilities. He has two himself. He lives in Danvers, and his family goes back to Salem Village."

"Salem Village," her father said in unison.

"Sir, the reason I'm here is because Jamie's in danger."

"Call me Reese. What kind of danger?"

"I overheard two men talking about how they were going to use a spell to capture her. One of them told the other guy the…unspeakable things he was going to do to her before turning her over to his boss for some—" he used air quote "—power thing."

Her mother's face paled, reminding her of when Tony got hit by a car while riding his bike and spent a week in the hospital.

Reese glanced at his wife before turning to his daughter. "Jamie, I think you should come back here where we can protect you better."

"Dad…power transfer rituals require a virgin." She waited for him to understand what she hadn't said. Heat rose in her cheeks. "I'm not."

His eyes slid to Theron.

"No, Dad. Not Theron." She couldn't believe her sex life was part of their discussion. "Anyway, if they figure that out, I'm afraid they'll snatch Abby instead. I don't want to endanger her."

Her mother's quiet voice drew her attention. "Maybe they don't know."

Jamie spread her hands in front of her. "Maybe I should put up a billboard, *Jamie Ballard is not a virgin.*"

Kathleen stiffened. "Jamie!"

"Sorry, Mom. If not for Theron, I would never know anyone was after me."

She squeezed Theron's thigh near his knee, and he wrapped his hand around hers.

She threw herself back against the chair, pulling free. "Why me? How do they know me?"

Her father reached for his wife's hand. "Nathan Proctor was well known in certain circles. They may have known he

49

had children."

Jamie leaned forward. "And waited for us to grow up?"

Reese shrugged. "We don't know enough about this, which is why you should come back home."

She glanced at Theron, needing his support. Her parents would feel they could protect her best. Most parents would think that.

Theron shrugged one shoulder. "It's up to you."

She leaned back, drew her knees to her chin and stared at the closed doors. If she stayed with her parents, she'd have two more people to protect her, and even Tony could help. But, it possibly exposed Abby. If these people already knew where she lived and she wasn't here, would Abby still be at risk? Maybe they only knew she lived in Rawlins. How many people in town would tell these strangers where she lived?

Reese leaned forward. "Jamie, you and Abby can be protected together."

She planted her feet on the floor and stood. "No. You protect Abby. I'll go back to Jason's house and hope that gives us enough time to find out what's going on before these guys figure out where I am."

Chapter 6

Theron woke to Jamie's scream. He bolted out of bed, and caught his foot in the sheet, falling on his hands. He yanked his foot twice before it was freed, then raced across the hall.

In the dim light of the bathroom nightlight, his eyes fell on Jamie, and then he scanned the room. She was alone, but thrashing.

He sat on the edge of the bed and rubbed her shoulder. "Jamie. Jamie, wake up!" He shook her shoulder a little, then ran his hand down her cheek. "Jamie, it's just a dream. Wake up."

Her eyes popped open and settled on him. "Theron!" She jackknifed into his arms. "He killed him! He…" A shiver passed through her.

Theron rubbed her back. "It was just a dream. Who killed who?"

"A gray haired man with almost black eyes. Evil radiated from him." She shivered again. "He killed that guy you overheard talking about hurting me. His name is—was Walt."

Theron grabbed her arms and pulled back from her, staring into her eyes. "You're sure? Did it feel like a premonition?"

"It was like…It was more vivid than a regular dream, so

yes. It was a premonition. Or I saw it as it happened." Her breathing slowed.

"Do you know why the guy killed him?" His fear for Jamie intensified. This man had no qualms about killing.

She squeezed her eyes shut for a second. "The old guy told him that he couldn't be trusted anymore because he planned to hurt me." Her voice choked. "The sacrifices always had more bruises than he'd expect when they were acquired and now he knew why." Tears shimmered.

"And Walt said, 'But you're going to kill them anyway, and I leave them virgins.' The old man backhanded him and said that I wasn't a sacrifice, and had to be treated carefully. Walt said he hadn't known, but he'd treat me right. The old guy told him it was too late and cut his throat. Blood gushed down his shirt." Her eyes squeezed closed and she shivered. "Ugh."

Theron pulled her close. Walt's fate didn't bother him at all. "At least the sadistic guy is gone or will be."

Somewhat reassured they didn't plan on killing her, he still worried about the reason they wanted to kidnap her.

He glanced at the clock. "It's two in the morning. You should probably try to get back to sleep. You're not likely to have that dream again."

Hers arms tightened around him. "Not alone."

It broke his heart that a dream had frightened her so much. "All right. Scoot over."

She moved away from him and put her head on the other pillow. He stretched out, but before he could put his head down, she spoke. "Under the covers."

It was exactly where he wanted to be, but not the reason. Lying beside her in friendship would be almost the hardest thing he'd ever done. He stood, lifted the covers and slid under. He buried his face in the pillow, filled with the scent of her shampoo and Jamie. He stretched out his hand to take hers, so even in sleep she'd know he was there. She gripped it and moved closer, until her hip bumped his then turned on her side, snuggling her head into his shoulder. He'd never been this physically close to her before, and it was for all the wrong reasons.

"Thank you."

"Not a problem." It was so much a problem. If he turned on his side, he could slide his knee between her thighs and feel her heat. He hoped her eyes were closed, because the little bit of light coming in the window would reveal his bulge under the blanket.

Theron listened to her breathing as it slowed and her body relaxed into sleep. She felt so right beside him and he hoped that soon, she'd be in his bed for all the right reasons. He rested his free hand on her waist and fell asleep.

***

Her warm pillow…moved. Jamie opened her eyes to see a male nipple inches away. Not a pillow. The memory from the middle of the night came back to her. The dream. Theron had come to protect her.

She'd always been comfortable in his presence, but cuddled up to him like this, with only his shorts on? On the edge of anxious, she worried that he would awaken when she moved away. That Theron dream made her want a whole lot more from him than what they'd shared in the past, and she didn't know how he felt about that.

His breathing changed and his hand rubbed up and down her back. She couldn't tell if he was trying to comfort her or if it was a hint of something else. They had a choice of two kinds of awkward. Two friends in bed, holding each other almost intimately, or two friends and one trying to turn it into a romantic interlude. There was the third, definitely not awkward option. They both wanted their friendship to become something more.

She chose option two, in hopes that it would become option three. She turned her head and kissed his chest. Two inches down, his nipple tempted her. She circled it with her tongue and he inhaled sharply and tightened his arm around her. She kissed and nibbled her way up his chest, over his scratchy neck, and to his lips.

His arms circled her, and one hand slipped into her hair, turning her head a bit as he deepened the kiss. If she'd known how good he could kiss, maybe she would have done it a long time ago.

She slid her leg over his and her knee bumped…yes! He wanted this, too.

He cupped her face and pushed her head back, staring into her eyes. "Jamie, are you sure?"

"Yes. Doing this with you is practically all I've thought about since I came home."

"What? You thought about this? I've been trying for a year to come up with a way for you to see me as more than a friend." He cupped her face. "Jamie, you're more dear to me than any friend ever."

A hum went through her chest. "Why didn't you tell me?"

One corner of his mouth tipped up. "You weren't ready. I'm not sure what changed, but I'm glad."

She dropped her eyes to his lips. "Um. I had this dream about making love with you. It was amazing and—" She gazed into his eyes. "I couldn't think of you as just a friend after that."

He gave her a quick kiss and dropped his head back. "We haven't been just friends for a long time." He started to slip out from under her. "I'm going to get a condom from my bag. Take that time to make sure this is what you want."

She snickered. "There are condoms in the nightstand."

He quirked an eyebrow and she shrugged. Without taking his eyes from hers, he reached into the drawer and pulled out a strip of condoms, tearing one off.

Once she'd become friends with Theron, she hadn't been interested in dating. Funny how she'd never seen him as date material until after the dream.

He slid out of his shorts. Dream Theron had nothing on the real one. His sexy chest flexed with every move. His warm skin pressed against hers. And watching him slip on the condom. Oh, my.

He tipped her head up, and she caught his smile. Yep. He noticed she'd been staring. His eyes were a warmer gold than normal. The way those eyes devoured her made her breath catch. He was her Theron. Her friend, about to become her lover. Nothing was more important than this.

That mouth, with the fuller bottom lip, hadn't been on hers enough. She licked her suddenly dry lips and felt his heartbeat kick up.

He pushed her to her back, and his kisses made her want so much more. His chest half covered hers, but her t-shirt separated them. She struggled pulling the hem up, and then he yanked the shirt over her head.

"Jamie." His hand trembled as he touched her breast. "I feel like I'm dreaming. I've wanted us to be closer for so long, but I didn't want to scare you away. I couldn't live without you in my life."

She pulled his head back down and mumbled against his lips. "It's not a dream." The dream kisses weren't half as good as real ones. And if that held true for the rest, she would combust.

His warm hand kneaded her breast and his callused thumb rubbed across her nipple. Each touch made her crave the next. She moaned.

His lips left hers and she started to protest until little nibbles trailed down her throat, sending shivers racing to her core. His warm mouth covered her nipple as his hand slipped beneath her panties. She arched and wrapped an arm around his head.

Her breath came in short bursts. Then his cool fingers slipped into her folds, and all the air whooshed out of her lungs and her stomach contracted. She gasped in a breath as tingles spread. His finger made lazy circles, but she didn't have a lazy response. Heat followed the tingles, then tiny flutters took over. They grew so intense, she curled her upper body around his head. Her whole body stiffened and almost ached. She shattered with a scream and fell back to the bed.

"Theron. I didn't know. Wow." Maybe she'd run around the block three times and forgot.

He tried to kiss her, but she couldn't catch her breath and tipped her head back. He kissed her jaw.

He chuckled. "Oh, it gets better." He levered himself over her and dropped one knee between hers and then the other.

She drew up her knees to hug his hips, pulled his head down and kissed him. How had she never felt this overpowering need for him before?

His hand slipped between them, and his length touched her entrance. She tensed until his fingers ran up her slick folds, setting off a whole new craving. They both moaned when he slipped in an inch. He started to pull back and she wrapped her legs around him. She needed more. He pushed in farther and retreated, and farther again. Then he was all the way in, and he stilled. She breathed in huffs, feeling so full, but it wasn't enough.

She wiggled and he pulled back only to surge in again, then set a slow rhythm. Glorious pressure mounted, and she lifted her hips to meet each thrust, needing a faster pace. His magical fingers seemed to know exactly the touch she needed. Little flutters turned into pulsing exhilaration.

Theron's head dropped into her neck. She couldn't keep up with his frenzied movements. She screamed as another orgasm shook her. He surged in and stiffened, then roared.

Jamie took deep breaths, trying to slow her breathing. She gasped as Theron rolled to the side, taking her with him.

He scattered tiny kisses on her forehead, nose, cheeks, and chin. She giggled.

"Baby, don't do that."

"Why?"

"I'm still inside you. That laugh tightened you around me."

She ducked her head. "Oh."

He lifted her chin with a finger. "I don't think you're ready for round three."

Just the thought of doing that again made her muscles clench.

He closed his eyes. "Mmm. Or maybe you are." He hugged her. "I'm going to shower, and make you breakfast. And then we're going to talk."

Chapter 7

After breakfast Theron dragged Jamie into the family room for the serious discussion they so much needed. Now they were in new territory, and he didn't want distractions, other than Jamie.

He sat on the couch, expecting her to snuggle next to him. Instead she left a cushion between them.

"What are you doing over there?" He scooted to the empty cushion and pulled her onto his lap.

She bit her lip. "I wasn't sure what—"

He kissed her and she wrapped her arms around his neck, relaxing against him.

He touched her chin. "That's better. I know we've been friends for so long it's hard to shift gears."

She bit her lip again. "But, what are we now? Friends with benefits?"

"What I *want* is for you to be my girlfriend." What she suggested seemed shallow for the way he felt. What he really wanted was for her to become his fiancé, but he thought it was too soon to propose.

"Um, okay. But can we pretend we were boyfriend-girlfriend before we had sex?"

He chuckled. "We made love. It wasn't *just* sex. And yes." He winked. "Don't you remember we had this boyfriend-girlfriend conversation last night?"

She laughed and kissed his cheek. "No. It totally slipped my mind. Thank you."

"Now that that's settled, we should talk about your dream."

She rubbed her nose on his cheek. "The one where we made love?"

"Would you tell me about that one?"

She buried her face in his neck. "It was pretty much what happened this morning, except…"

"Except what?"

Jamie drew in a breath. "Forget I said that."

He pushed her to create a space between them, so he could look at her. "Except what?"

She closed her eyes. "Except I didn't know it was you until the end."

"You made love with a stranger?"

She glared at him. "Hey! It was a dream. You can't help who you dream about, and I felt like I knew him." She pushed his shoulder. "Besides, I'm sure you've had your share of sex dreams. This was my first."

He smirked. "Guilty. But the past year have all been you."

She straightened up. "You said you didn't have that dream."

"I didn't have a *premonition* dream. I had lots of fantasy dreams."

She blushed. "I guess you didn't need a premonition dream."

He bracketed her face with his hands and kissed her. "Nope. Not at all."

He settled back against the couch with her head tucked under his chin. "I hate to change the subject, but we need to talk about your nightmare."

She sighed. "What do you want to know?"

"The old man said you weren't a sacrifice. What other reason would they want you?" He tipped his head and waited.

A few seconds past before she gazed at him. "I can't think of any. Maybe Mom knows. Do you think they gave up since he killed that guy?"

He wished he could tell her it was over. He released a long breath. "No. I think he'll hire another accomplice to assist the jerk who's left." He nuzzled his nose into Jamie's hair and breathed in her scent. "You're important to him."

She shivered. "I don't want to be important to a killer."

Theron snuggled her to his chest. Having serial killer birth parents must have been rough for her. He wondered when she'd found out. "Do you think that guy could have some association with Nathan Proctor?"

The pain in her face made him wish he hadn't asked.

"I don't see how he could."

"Is there anything else you remember? Did the old guy look familiar? What did the room look like?"

She wrinkled her brow. "I didn't recognize him. He leaned against a desk and Walt sat in a wooden chair in front of him. There was a picture on the wall of a leafless tree, and a fire in front of it with three shadowy people standing around it. I thought the flames would consume the tree." She shrugged. "Sorry. That wasn't very helpful."

"Why don't you give your mom a call later and see if they come up with anything."

"Okay."

He pushed off the couch, and let her slide down his side. "And now we're working on self-defense."

Her eyebrows hiked up. "Taekwondo? But you've been teaching me that for years."

"And you've made a game of it. Serious training starts now." This would be the first time they worked out together

60

in a couple of months. He was afraid he'd be the one making it a game. A sex game. He shook his head and ran a hand through his hair. No. It was deadly serious. He'd push her hard. The same way he trained the teens for competition.

He nudged her. "Go put on work-out clothes. I'll meet you in the backyard."

She hurried from the room and he headed to the dining area. He opened the French door and studied the yard. Fortunately, it was private. A high wood fence separated it from the neighbors, and totally enclosed the area. No passing kidnappers would see Jamie.

Moments after he stepped out onto the deck, Jamie came up behind him and placed a hand on his back. Yeah, he might have a hard time staying in Taekwondo mode.

He grabbed her hand. "Let's go." He stopped in the center of the yard and faced her. "You know the routine. We start with warm-ups."

She followed his every move. Theron had always enjoyed watching Jamie go through the poses. She flowed through each move with grace, having done dance as a child. Now, however, he imagined her naked, seductively dancing for him. He stared over her head as he finished up, needing to think of her as a student. Not likely. Continuous reminding that this could protect Jamie from kidnappers might get him through.

He held his hands up. "Okay. We'll do a review of what you know and then start adding more advanced self-defense moves."

With minimal instruction, Jamie moved through the kicks, hits and blocks. Then Theron moved onto ways she might be taken, and showed her how to counter each move.

Jamie threw him down and landed on him.

He stared into her mesmerizing, blue eyes. "You should be running."

"I know. But I couldn't resist." She kissed him

It wasn't like he hadn't been thinking about it for the last half-hour. He became a willing participant, but when he almost reached the point of no return, he pushed her up. His breaths came in rasps, kiss induced or from the workout, he couldn't tell. "Fifteen more minutes, and then I'm all yours. Right here. Like this."

Her eyes widened and he almost laughed. Her eyes darted around the yard. "Here?"

"Sure. It's private. Who's going to know?"

She pushed up and stood over him. "Me?"

He got to his feet. "Okay. We'll decide in fifteen minutes." It would be easy to make her forget where she was.

***

They settled into a routine. The best parts were the nights or after training, when they made love.

After breakfast, Theron lifted weights in the exercise room he'd found in the basement while Jamie punched and kicked a weight bag. Then they went into the backyard and worked on her Taekwondo skills. She'd progressed more in the week they'd been intensely practicing than in the entire time he'd trained with her. It had gotten easier to keep his mind on the training after the first time. She was good enough to protect herself from an untrained mugger, but might have trouble if trained men came after her.

He held up his fist and she stopped. "Let's throw something else in the mix. How well can you control your heat generation?"

She shrugged. "It's been years since I exploded my coffee cup. I haven't burned anyone since I accidentally burned Jason, when I was twelve."

"I wish I had some kind of fire suit." He scanned the yard

and saw a pile of branches beside the fence at the back. He hurried to the pile, chose two thick, short branches and returned to Jamie. He dropped one and held up the other. "This isn't ideal, but I want you to pretend this is an arm coming at you. Grab it and give it all the heat you can."

He swung the two-foot branch, not too fast. Jamie wrapped one hand around it and within seconds, smoke rose from between her fingers. She released it, leaving a singed handprint on the bark. He came at her straight on, as a fist would strike her face. She caught the end, wincing at the force, but held on until he yanked it back as smoke swirled.

She didn't let go soon enough and was overbalanced. He grabbed her wrist, spinning her back into his front, swinging the stick in front of her, as if to box her in. She grabbed it. This time, the wood burst into flames and Theron tossed it on the green grass, stomping on it until the flames were extinguished. Hopefully, the grass wasn't permanently damaged.

He pulled her tight, wishing she didn't have this threat hanging over her. That they could spend their time getting used to their new relationship. "Okay. That's enough."

She sagged in his arms and he turned her around.

"You did great. Combine Taekwondo with your hot little hands and you've got a chance."

She buried her face in his neck. "Theron, I never expected to use that ability to attack anyone."

"You're not attacking. You're defending." He had to make sure she saw it that way, or she might not work hard enough for herself.

"And my lightning ability is just a stupid trick, but now I keep thinking of ways to use it against other people. And…"

"And what, baby?"

She shook her head.

Theron pulled back and took her face in his hands. "If

you're captured, I want you to use all your abilities, any way you need to, to get away. No ability is evil if it's used for a good cause. And your escaping is the best cause."

He tried to gauge her reaction. "Do you believe me?"

She bit her lip and stared at him. He wished she would confide in him. She must have an ability that scared her.

Finally, she nodded. "Okay. If I'm captured, I'll use all my abilities to escape, including my smarts."

He hugged her, pulled in a lungful of air and released it in a rush. "Jamie, what other ability do you have?"

Her eyes widened and she stiffened, then turned her head, relaxing as she rested it against his chest. "I can't talk about it."

"We might develop better defense if I knew."

She shook her head.

He dropped his shoulders. She did have another ability, but didn't trust him enough to reveal it.

***

Jamie couldn't believe how fast two weeks could fly. The intense training they'd been doing seemed like it was for nothing. No attempts had been made. It almost seemed as if the dream about Walt dying had ended the search. She began doubting it was real, but Theron pushed her daily, not backing down.

Jason and Shauna would be home within a few of hours. She and Theron had made sure to clean the house and he'd bought groceries. She'd even put a pot roast in the oven.

She leaned against Theron's chest, surveying the family room. Everything in place. Theron had suggested they move their things to the furthest bedroom from Jason and Shauna's, in case they were staying. The newlywed couple probably wanted to continue their honeymoon, so she wasn't so sure it mattered where their bags were.

Theron hugged her and whispered in her ear. "You want to practice in the backyard?"

She twisted around and placed a palm on each side of his head, pulling it down for a kiss. "Practice what?"

He chuckled. "Well, I was thinking Taekwondo and heat, but I could go for bodies and heat on that chaise lounge."

She grinned and pushed out of his arms, racing to the kitchen door. On the deck, she shed her clothes and sprawled on the lounge chair. She squeaked when Theron lifted the foot and wheeled the chair out of direct sight of the door.

He leaned down and kissed her. "Just in case the plane's early."

Jamie enjoyed watching him strip and put on a condom. He lowered over her then nibbled her neck, making her squirm, but once his lips found hers, she couldn't hold back a moan.

Part of his weight rested on his left arm, but most of his body was gloriously pressed against hers. His right hand cupped her face, and he pulled back.

"Jamie, I love you." He pecked her lips. "I have for a long time."

She bit her lip. "I'm sorry I didn't notice. I've loved you, but not that way, until a couple weeks ago."

He kissed her again. "It's okay. It had to be the right time." He grinned. "And I was going to make sure that this was the right time."

His warm lips touched hers as his hand trailed down her throat to her breast. His fingers worked their magic as her tongue dueled with his. He could have stepped out of one of the romance books her mom had in the library. They'd seemed so over-the-top sensual until Theron touched her. This was better than anything she'd read in those books.

His hand slipped lower and touched her most sensitive

spot. It was more than the sensations or the excitement. Her heart seemed to expand with each touch. Each caress showed how much he cared and that his foremost thought was her pleasure.

She couldn't catch her breath, and turned her head. He nibbled her ear. Waves of pleasure shook her as he joined their bodies. He withdrew and drove deeper.

Each time he pulled back, she pulled him in, until he stiffened above her.

"My Jamie." He dropped down on her and then shifted.

She shrieked when the lounge chair tipped sideways, then giggled as she landed on top of Theron.

The patio door flew open and Jason stepped out, slapping a hand over his eyes. "I could have gone my whole life not seeing my sister's naked backside." He stepped back into the house. "Come on in when you're dressed."

Jamie dropped her head to Theron's chest. "Oh, my, God. I can't believe that happened. They shouldn't be here yet."

Theron ran a hand down her spine, making her shiver. "I guess he knows what we've been doing. He's not going to threaten me, is he?"

She nipped his lips. "Don't worry about it. He already knew you'd be here."

His eyes widened. "How could he know?"

She bit her lip. "Ah, you know my dream? He kind of wormed it out of me. He believed you'd be coming here more than I did."

"And he approved?"

She shrugged. "That's why I'm house sitting."

"O-okaaay. We'd better get dressed."

She tried to make it sound like there was nothing to it, but she still had to face her brother. And Theron had to surreptitiously dispose of a condom in the kitchen trash.

Jamie preceded Theron into the house. Jason leaned

against the kitchen island, talking to Shauna.

Jamie ran and wrapped her arms around her brother. "Jason. I'm glad you're back." She poked him in the chest. "But you could have given a heads up that you'd be early."

He chuckled.

Theron washed his hands at the kitchen sink, and joined her and shook Jason's hand. "Nice to see you, Jason."

"Likewise." He smirked, and drew Shauna close to him. "And this is Shauna, my wife." He kissed his wife's forehead, and looked down at her. "I still get a thrill saying that."

Jamie glanced at Shauna. "Dinner's almost ready. Want to help me?"

"Sure. It smells delicious."

Over pot roast, potatoes, onions and carrots, Jamie and Theron brought Jason and Shauna up to speed on the threat against Jamie.

Jason tapped his finger on the table. "I wonder if my friend, Mark, can find this Walt guy."

She remembered Jason used to work with Mark, but didn't know what Mark did. "Jason, that's impossible." Jamie couldn't hide her exasperation. "If I were an artist, I could draw a picture. And how would finding a dead guy help?"

"We could find out who his associates were. It might get us closer to who wants you."

"Speaking of drawing," Theron said, "do you know a police sketch artist I could work with? I saw both men. Maybe Mark could find their pictures in a database somewhere."

Jason nodded. "Excellent idea. We can distribute it to the Rawlins police and have them looking for this creep." He squinted. "I'll have Mom and Dad fortify the protection spell, so this guy can't detect you in the house. We'll keep the security system active at all times." He glared at Theron. "If it *had* been on, you would have heard when we came through the front door."

Theron shrugged one shoulder, not seeming embarrassed like she felt. "We turn it on at night."

"All. The. Time." Jason stared down Theron and Jamie until they agreed.

Jamie bit her lip. "Jason, does that mean you don't want Theron and me to go home?"

Jason pushed back in his seat. "Of course not. Why would you ask?"

"Well, you're newlyweds. I figured you'd want to be alone."

Jason reached across the table and took her hand. "Jamie, you're safer with me. Those guys have Mom and Dad's address. They'll probably stake the place out."

She tensed. "But, what about Abby?" She'd figured the guys would just wander around town, looking for her. Not that they'd know where to look.

Jason shook his head. "It sounds like they specifically want you, so they won't go after Abby. And, you don't look alike. But she's been warned, just in case. Right?"

"Yeah. Mom and Dad were going to talk to her and Tony. Oh, you should probably call Mom to let her know you're home. I'm surprised she hasn't called here already."

"I called while you and Shauna were putting dinner on the table, and told her I'd let her know if you were still staying here or going home."

She glanced at Theron and back to Jason. "Thanks for letting us stay. And you, too, Shauna. I get to avoid that, *But, Mom. Theron shared my room at Jason's* talk."

Jason kissed Shauna's cheek. "You'd be surprised. Just tell her about your dream, and she'd probably back right off."

"You're kidding. I'm not telling Mom about that dream."

Jason chuckled. "You know Mom and Dad met in a

dream."

"Yeah, but they only kissed."

Jason grinned. "Well, Shauna dreamed about me before we met. And I had a dream about her the night we met. And those dreams were more like yours."

She leaned forward, almost putting her hand in her plate. "You told Mom about having sex with Shauna in your dream?"

Shauna's cheeks turned pink. "Jason."

He chuckled. "Not details. Just that it was X-rated. I think she started planning grandbabies."

Jamie put a hand over her eyes. It would have been better to have this discussion alone with Jason. She glanced at Theron and wondered about his silly smile.

The discussion didn't seem to bother him. "Hey, I didn't get to have one of those dreams, but I'm sure it wouldn't have been as good as the real thing."

The heat of her cheeks made her think that maybe hers were very bright.

Now Jason had the silly smile. "Looks like you didn't need the prompting."

Was she the only one bothered by this discussion? "I'm going to get the dishwasher loaded." She picked up some dishes and headed to the kitchen.

Shauna was on her heels with her hands full.

Chapter 8

Theron came at Jamie and she shifted, throwing him over her hip. Every time she did it, she flinched, afraid he'd land wrong and break his neck or arm. She spun around to watch him get up from the grass, catching her breath.

He rubbed his hands down his legs. "You do know that's the point you should run."

"Well, yeah, but then we couldn't do it again and you'd be chasing me all over the yard."

He wiggled his eyebrows. "And I'd catch you." He picked up one of the thick sticks. "Let's do heat now." He swung the stick.

She'd gotten pretty good at this. Better than Taekwondo alone. She grabbed the wood as it came at her and heated it.

Theron yanked it from her hands.

"That's great, Jamie." They both turned at Jason's voice. "I didn't think about you using that for self-defense." He held up his arm where a dark oval marred the skin. She still felt bad about it.

Jason held up a hand. "Hold on a sec. I think I've got something to help." He disappeared into the house. A minute later, he came down to them with a coat thrown over his arm, and handed it to Theron. "Here. Put this on. It's made of wool and won't burn. It should keep most of the heat away, too." He sprinted back to the deck and sat.

Theron put the coat on and zipped it. He was a similar size to Jason, so it was a good fit. "Go easy until we see how this protects me."

Jamie turned her back to him and he lunged at her, wrapping his arms around her waist. One of her arms was caught under his, but with the other she gripped his arm, being careful to temper her heat.

His breath tickled her ear. "Turn it up a bit."

She notched up the heat, not nearly what she'd done to the stick, but closer.

"Good. I can feel it. A little more." He released her and spun her around. His hands came for her throat and she gripped an arm in each hand, and pushed them to the side as she knocked him with her hip.

This put the training more into perspective, rather than going for a stick. That might prove helpful.

After more defense moves, she threw him and he stayed on the ground. She sunk beside him. He wrapped a hand behind her neck and pulled her down for a kiss. If he'd done anything else, she probably would have punched him, but this definitely wasn't about fighting.

He drew her head back an inch. "Want to go shower?"

She slowly nodded, and hoped he meant with him.

He chuckled. "Good. Because this coat is like a sauna." It still surprised her how fast he could leap up. He took her hand to help her.

They turned toward the house and Jason clapped. "Jamie, I'm amazed." His face clouded. "I wish I'd thought to train Shauna. Maybe she wouldn't have gotten kidnapped."

Shauna stepped out of the house and wrapped her arms around him from behind. "But it turned out all right."

"You saved yourself." There was pride in Jason's voice.

She kissed his cheek. "Only because you were close

enough so I could think."

Jamie hadn't known about the kidnapping. "Oh, Shauna. How awful."

Shauna closed her eyes and Jason drew her in front of him, enclosing her in his arms. She leaned her head onto her husband's chest. "My ex-fiancé didn't want to give me up."

Jason kissed Shauna's cheek. "No more thinking about that. Let's have lunch."

***

Jamie and Shauna worked together pulling out plates and food for sandwiches and putting them on the kitchen island. They'd worked well together doing meal preparations over the past two weeks.

The security system notified them that the front door had been opened. The women stared at each other, wide-eyed.

Shauna crept to the doorway. "Jason!" She disappeared in a flurry.

Jamie stopped in the doorway and leaned against it. Her brother held Shauna in his arms as they kissed. If a stranger saw them, they'd think he'd returned from a month's long trip. It pleased her that Jason had found a woman who loved him so much.

Jason had been going into his office every day, taking care of small jobs he'd lined up while on his honeymoon. Today was the first day he'd come home before lunch.

Theron rushed up from the basement and came to a quick stop, his eyes on the couple. His shoulders dropped. "Just in time for lunch."

They entered the kitchen, and each prepared their own sandwich at the kitchen island. Shauna poured glasses of tea and Jason grabbed a bag of chips. They sat at the dining table.

They chattered halfway through lunch before Jason ended their merriment. "I heard from the police today. They spotted that guy from your drawing. He was with another guy."

Jamie lost her appetite as her stomach clenched into knots. No wonder he'd come home early. "In Rawlins? Did they arrest him?"

Jason shook his head. "As far as they know, he hasn't done anything wrong."

Jamie had been able to push thoughts of kidnapping out of her mind. She practiced with Theron. It was more intense than it used to be, but still fun. She'd seen Jason every day, after so many years of two or three visits a year. And Shauna. Jamie could see why Jason had fallen in love with her. She was becoming a wonderful friend.

Now, the fear was closing in. Half the time was gone for that power thing someone needed her for. It was surprising the guys hadn't shown up before now. Maybe they'd been around and the police hadn't spotted them before.

Theron squeezed her hand. "Anything on who he is?"

Jason grimaced. "No. Nothing. Want to go look? We can rough them up a little. See if they crack."

Theron glanced at her. "I don't want to leave Jamie alone, especially since we know they're close."

Her heart pounded, her fear doubling. She didn't want Theron to leave, but she wanted it over. If talking to those men could get the information they needed, it might be worth the worry. "Theron's the only one who's seen him. And I don't want him meeting up with two of them alone." She blew out a shuddering breath. "I'll be safe here with Shauna." She hoped. How would anybody know she was here?

***

Jamie paced the living room as Shauna watched her from

73

the couch. Jamie stopped in front of her. "Aren't you the least bit worried?"

"A little. But I know Jason can take care of himself. He's good at this stuff."

Jamie resumed her pacing. "Theron can, too. Unless they have guns." She threw her hands in the air. "God! Why did I think that?"

The doorbell rang and both their eyes swiveled to the door. Shauna jumped off the couch and grabbed her arm. "Don't answer that."

Jamie bit her lip. "But what if Theron got hurt and it's the police?"

Shauna stared at her for a few seconds. "I'll peek. If they see me, they still won't know you're here." She tipped her head just enough for one eye to peek out the window beside the door. "It's Abby. I wonder what she's doing here."

Shauna unlatched the door and fell on her butt when it was flung the rest of the way open. A man stood in the doorway, holding a knife to Abby's throat. She looked dwarfed, pressed against the large man's chest, her eyes wide with fear. Hadn't Shauna seen the man? But she still would have opened the door because Abby was in danger.

Shauna scrambled up and Jamie stood beside her.

"Don't hurt her." Jamie had tried to protect her little sister by keeping away from home. The guy could cut Abby's throat before dropping her and grabbing Jamie. And Shauna. Would they hurt her, too?

Jamie's legs shook, barely holding her up. "Please…"

A second man walked in, the one that Theron had described for the police picture. "We won't harm her if you come with us."

There was no choice, but believe them. If they'd held the knife to her own throat she would have known what to do. With Abby at risk, she had no hope of fighting them. All the training Theron had given her was useless.

The first man uttered some words, and Abby slumped in his arms. He pushed her to the floor.

"No!" Jamie lunged for her sister, but the second man grabbed Jamie, trapping her arms against her body, then plunged a needle into her neck. As the room went gray, she saw a matching needle shoved into Shauna's neck.

***

Theron stepped dejectedly out of Jason's car. "Let's try again tomorrow. At least we know people weren't telling them anything."

He climbed the steps behind Jason and waited for him to unlock the door. Jason didn't immediately step in and Theron tried to look around him.

"Shauna! Abby!" Jason raced into the house and squatted down between the prone women.

Theron clutched his constricted throat. "Jamie!" He could feel that she wasn't there, and something had happened with her neck. "Jamie!" He shouldn't have left her.

The only way to find out what happened would be to question Shauna and Abby.

He squatted beside Jamie's sister, and rubbed her cheek. "Abby. Wake up." He took her hand and spoke louder. "Abby. Please wake up." The air around Abby felt heavy. "I think she's been spelled."

Jason lifted an eyebrow. "You can tell?"

"Yeah."

"Can you check Shauna?"

Theron skipped over to Shauna's other side and touched her face. He shook his head. "Not spelled." He noticed a scratch on her neck that appeared to end in a puncture. "Look here." He pointed. "She's been drugged. I wonder why they aren't the same."

Jason touched Shauna's necklace. "If they tried to spell her, it wouldn't have worked because she's protected."

Shauna moaned and put her hand to her head.

Jason leaned over her, gently rubbing her face. "Shauna, honey."

She blinked and seemed to focus, then launched into his arms. "Jason. They took Jamie. They showed up with Abby and held a knife to her throat. They didn't give Jamie a choice." It was then she noticed Abby and threw herself across Jason. "Abby!" She ran her fingers down Abby's cheek. "They spelled her. I couldn't understand the words." She squeezed Jason's arm. "Call your mom. She'll know what to do."

Theron needed answers. He wanted to race out and find Jamie, but he didn't know where to go. He stood and paced. At a time when she needed him most, he was helpless. "Shauna, when did this happen?"

She rubbed her forehead. "I don't know. About fifteen minutes after you left?"

He roared in rage. Jamie had been missing for nearly three hours. She could be out of state, or on a plane to the other side of the country. He heard Jason's voice on the phone and blocked it. He'd finally been able to tell Jamie he loved her, and heard the same from her. He'd held her in his arms only to have her ripped away from him. He couldn't stop the tear that ran down his cheek, but angrily brushed it away. He would do whatever was necessary to get her back.

Chapter 9

Jamie groaned. The worst headache ever pounded in her temples. No matter the time, she'd stay in bed until she felt better. She pulled the covers over her head.

The sheets didn't smell right. She squished them to her nose and sniffed. Not her mother's detergent or Shauna's. She threw the covers back and stared at a drop ceiling and fluorescent lights.

Kidnapped. The vice in her head became unbearable as her heart pumped up the pressure with staccato beats. She pushed up, drawing her legs to her chest, finding herself in the center of a double bed. She dropped her chin to her knees, relieved she was fully dressed. Jeez. She never thought she'd be in a position to have rape cross her mind.

That horrible man had held a knife to Abby's throat. Her sister's blood could have been spilled in front of her. The man spoke a spell before thrusting Abby away, without slashing her with the knife. Jamie hoped that meant that Abby was alive, and it hadn't been a death spell. But wouldn't he have used the knife if his intent was to kill Abby? Unless he didn't want Jamie to know he'd killed her. Jamie covered her mouth to hold in a cry, and hoped her sister was alive.

She touched the sore spot on her neck where she'd been

injected. They'd injected Shauna, too. She hoped it was the same thing she'd been given, and that Shauna was all right now. She squeezed her eyes shut, imagining the pain Jason would go through if he'd lost Shauna. A tear trickled out as her heart constricted.

And Theron. He would feel as if he'd failed her. It wasn't his fault. He'd trained her, protected her as much as he could.

Slowly, she lifted her head. The headache had lessened a bit. She scanned the windowless room. A commercial clock on the wall read ten-ten. She didn't know if it was morning or night.

She reached behind her, through the metal spindles of the headboard, and placed her palm on the wall. It felt cool and damp. A basement prison.

They hadn't really hurt her. Yet. Her breath quickened. She still didn't know her captors' plans. The summer solstice was days away. Her arms trembled and she tightened them around her legs. The solstice and equinox played a huge role in the human sacrifices her birth parents had performed. Whatever the reason she'd been taken, dark magic was involved.

Jamie glared at the steel door with a too small window across from her. She'd never break out that way. Through an open door to her right she saw a bathroom sink. At least they'd given her amenities. It wasn't quite a dungeon.

Keys rattled against the door. No. Jamie sucked in a breath. She wasn't ready to face whatever was on the other side. Her heart raced.

Maybe they'd been watching and knew she was awake and would take her somewhere to be killed. That man in the dream had said she wasn't a sacrifice, but it didn't mean she wouldn't die a different way.

She hugged her legs tighter, her breath coming in quick pants. No. She couldn't defend herself huddled in a ball.

Theron had taught her better than this. She uncurled her tense body, and stood on the bed, arms ready at her sides, as the door opened. So what if her hands trembled.

She caught the icy eyes of a man before he pushed another man into the room and slammed the door closed. The keys rattled again.

The man landed on his hands and knees, then sat back on his butt.

She dropped to the bed. "Adam! What are you doing here?" It made no sense that her kidnappers had brought someone she knew.

His blue eyes widened, and he ran a hand through his dark hair. "Jamie? What are you doing here? Are you all right? Did they hurt you?" He scrambled up, and took a step toward her.

She gasped, panic surging forward. Adam had been in some of her classes at UMass Boston. She'd even gone on a couple dates with him her first year, but for him to be in this place with her was too strange to comprehend.

He paused, scanned the room and walked to an overstuffed chair, dropping into it, bumping the side table that sat between it and the matching chair. His wide shoulders filled his olive green t-shirt.

Jamie was on edge, that was all. "I'm all right. So far." She scooted up, leaned against the uncomfortable headboard, and forced herself to relax. At least she wasn't alone in this. She examined the room, wondering if someone spied on them. She didn't see any cameras. A glance at the door found no one staring in through the small window.

She studied Adam. He seemed relaxed, laid back in the chair with his feet extended in front of him. He touched his jaw, drawing her attention to the blossoming bruise there.

She tucked her feet under the blankets. "Do you know where we are? I was unconscious when they brought me."

"No. I woke up as they hauled me down some stairs." He shifted in the chair. "I'm going to have bruises for a while."

She drew the blankets up to her waist. It shouldn't have made her feel better, but maybe her subconscious thought she was half hidden like this. "What day is it?" She didn't know if she'd been out for a short time or if she'd slept the night through.

"I think it's Friday. It doesn't feel like I was out that long."

All night. "Do you think it's a coincidence that we know each other?"

Adam crossed his arms. "No. It's got to mean something. Is it because we both went to UMass?"

She gave a dry chuckle. "Along with sixteen-thousand other students? Not likely." She squinted at him. She never once thought he might have abilities, but maybe…"Where are you from?"

"I grew up in Boston."

"But that's not where you were born?"

Adam frowned. "No. I was born in Salem."

Jamie covered her mouth. She'd half expected it, but it was still a shock to hear that they had a connection.

His eyebrows rose. "Were you born in Salem, too?"

She pushed her hair behind her ear. "No. But my ancestors came from Salem Village."

"Ancestors? You're not talking grandparents, are you?"

Normally, she didn't like to even think about her ancestors, but she wouldn't have to say much. "No. They settled Rawlins in 1693."

"After the witch trials?"

She nodded. "Yeah. It's a long story." He had to have abilities, too. They weren't taken because they knew each other. People were protective of their abilities with outsiders, but they needed to figure this out. "So, what's your ability?"

Adam ran his hands to the ends of the armrests. "You mean like, am I musical or do I excel in math?"

Even though she expected his caginess, she couldn't hold back her exasperation. "No. Can you leap a building in a single bound? Can you see through walls? Can you lift something without touching it?"

He chuckled. "You think I have super powers?"

"Yeah." She waited. He'd crossed his arms again, unwilling to cooperate. The smile on his lips hadn't reached his eyes. He wanted her to think he thought the question was funny, but he knew what she meant.

Maybe if she offered one of hers first, he'd give in. She gave another glance around the room before she held up her hands, fingers spread. "I can warm things with my hands. I didn't need a microwave in my dorm room because I could put my hands under my plate or around my cup and heat up the food or drink."

He leaned forward. "Wow. That's a useful skill."

She waited and stared. "You're not surprised? Not going to call me a freak?"

"No."

She sat straighter. "Why is that?"

He dropped back, but remained stiff. "All right! I have precognition."

She frowned. He wasn't going to give her a real ability. "Everybody with abilities can do that."

He rolled his eyes. "Most people have the occasional precognitive dream. I get flashes of premonition, and can put myself in a trance and make a prediction any time. Unfortunately, I can't do it for my own future, or I would have seen this coming."

She held her hands up as if to push him away. "Don't tell me mine. I don't want to know." No way would she want to hear how she'd die in the near future.

"I won't do it if you're not willing. And I've found that if someone is really against it, any images I get are too fuzzy to make out."

"Good." She leaned forward. "I had a precognitive dream. One of the men originally sent to kidnap me was killed by the man in charge. The head guy found out that the kidnapper was going to hurt me, so he told the kidnapper I was not a sacrifice and killed him."

His eyes widened. "Sacrifice? Good news you're not." He glanced toward the door. "I hope that goes for me, too."

"Only somewhat good." She sighed. "We could suffer a lot of pain and torture without dying." A shiver passed through her.

***

Theron pushed the barbell up and slowly lowered it to his chest. In his mind, the ceiling had all but disappeared with his thoughts on Jamie. Two days and they were no closer to finding her.

The police had called Jason the day before. Someone had gotten suspicious when the kidnappers had asked them about Jamie, and had written down their license plate number. They'd turned it in after hearing about her disappearance. It was a dead end. The plates had been stolen from a car in a neighboring town.

Mark was checking all his sources, but nothing related to Jamie or weird happenings had turned up. Jason had checked some other sources he wouldn't name, but nothing came of it.

Theron could sense Jamie lived, but nothing more. At least, he had that. It had surprised him when he felt that connection after she was taken, never having experienced it with anyone before. If only it gave him an advantage, some way to track her. He'd gone out, driven miles and miles in each direction, but there'd been no change in intensity.

He pushed the weight up with enough force to smash heads at the thought that Jamie could be hurting. Lowering the weight, he wished he was drawing her into his arms instead. They had to find her unharmed, but the longer it took, the more likely they wouldn't find her at all.

"No!" They *would* find her. He roared and shoved the weight up again. He couldn't live in a world without Jamie. A twisting pain already filled his heart. It wouldn't survive if he felt her death.

He grunted and worked the weights harder. The last push nearly did him in, and he strained to lower the bar into its rack.

He dropped his hands to the floor and closed his eyes, stretching out his senses, hoping that this time it would be different, but the sense remained a tiny flicker with no direction to find her.

Chapter 10

Jamie stretched in the dark. It felt like morning, but with no windows, she couldn't tell for sure. The night before, the overhead lights had turned off around eleven. She didn't know yet what time they came on.

She wished she could strike the building with lightning, but she didn't know where in the building she was. It would be best to strike the other side of the building and hope the guards would let them out to escape the fire. She didn't want to die in a fire if they didn't release her, so she couldn't take the chance.

A dim nightlight lit the bathroom, the door ajar. Just enough light to make it there. Sleep wouldn't return, so she got up to take a shower.

The doors on the vanity cabinet had been removed. On one side, wood fibers stuck out from the screw holes, as if the door had been torn off. Maybe someone had tried to use if for a weapon, so the kidnapper must have removed the other door.

Extra shampoo and body wash bottles sat inside the cabinet, as well as a couple of packages of sanitary pads. That was an uncomfortable find, considering Adam would see them, too. And a scary sign that someone planned on keeping her there a while.

She adjusted the temperature of the shower, and stepped in. Her thoughts went to Theron as the water flowed over her. They'd had many showers together. She imagined his soapy hands sliding across her skin, and his kisses on her shoulders and neck. She always dried off feeling warmer than when she went in. Maybe he was showering right now, having the same fantasies. She dropped her forehead to the wall and took gulping breaths. She'd get through this and back to him, somehow.

She finished up and put back on the t-shirt and underwear she'd worn.

A dresser sat beside the bathroom door, full of clothes for her and Adam. It was embarrassing that someone had gotten her bra size right. She hadn't found pajamas in the clothes they'd left her, so she'd used a t-shirt that had been in one of Adam's drawers. She didn't want to think about whether the lack of pajamas was an oversight, or if they wanted her naked at night.

It was a weird kidnapping. They were almost treated like guests, except they couldn't leave the room. Lunch and dinner had been good, brought in by one man while another stood beside the door with his hand on a holstered gun.

Maybe it was a bad thing that their faces hadn't been covered. She'd read that kidnappers who intended on releasing their hostages usually wanted to remain anonymous. However she looked at it, she was screwed.

Although afraid of what would happen to her, the fear lessened with Adam nearby. He didn't seem worried, but maybe he was good at hiding it.

She finished in the bathroom and walked halfway to the bed as light filled the room. Exactly seven o'clock. A glance at Adam found him still asleep. She shook her head. He looked so uncomfortable. He'd turned the two upholstered chairs to face each other, and curled up in one with his legs on the other.

She grabbed clothes and returned to the bathroom to change. As she came back out, Adam stretched and groaned. His blanket had slipped off, revealing shoulders stretching his t-shirt and muscled legs below the shorts.

A knock on the door startled her, as well as the muffled voice. "Stand back."

Jamie stayed put, assuming she was far enough away. Were they bringing another meal or would they take away one of them? She tensed, ready to fight if it was only one guard. A key turned in the lock and the door swung open. A tall, broad man with blond hair brought in a tray with two covered plates, two cups and orange juice. Just the scent of coffee made her feel more awake. He set the tray on the table and removed the tray from supper. A dark haired man with a crooked nose stood in the doorway, his eyes going from her to Adam, his hand resting on a holstered gun.

The blond man turned back at the door and stared at Jamie. "I'll be back at eight-thirty to take you to the gym, and you"— he turned to Adam—"at nine-thirty."

After the door closed behind him, she raised her eyebrows at Adam. "Apparently, we get to exercise, but not together." At least, she hoped they'd exercise in the gym and not be subjected to torture.

She strode to the table and lifted a lid on one plate. Pancakes and sausages. What she needed the most was coffee. She wrapped her hands around one cup, lifted it to her nose and pulled in a whiff. Perfect. She took a few sips. Exactly what she needed. She froze. Would they drug the food or drink? The coffee tasted normal, but maybe she wouldn't be able to detect drugs. The previous day's meals seemed okay. Except she'd fallen asleep pretty quickly after dinner, but that could have been because she'd been exhausted by her hyper emotions.

She shrugged and started to eat. She'd pay attention to how she felt. In a sense, she cooperated since she ate as they expected, but she needed to keep her strength up, in case the guards slipped up.

Adam joined her, lifting the lid off his food. He sniffed his coffee before drinking. He must be wondering about drugs, too. He rolled his head back and forth.

"Tonight, I'll sleep in the chair and you can have the bed."

His eyebrows rose. "You're sure? I'd kind of like to stretch out."

"Yeah. You looked like a pretzel."

He rolled his shoulders. "I felt like one. I still do. That gym time, if that's really what it is, should do me good."

Jamie stiffened. Her passing thought, verbalized, made it sound more likely. "You don't think that's what it is?"

He shrugged. "I don't know. I don't know why we're here, so I don't know why they'd give us a place to exercise."

She forced out a breath. "I wondered that, too."

Adam reached across the table and took her hand. "I wish they'd let us go together. I hate them taking you on your own."

Jamie slipped her fingers from his. "Thanks. But I don't think that's going to happen."

They finished eating in silence.

Before the guard returned, Jamie put on the athletic shoes she'd worn when she was kidnapped.

"Step back from the door." Keys rattled at the door and it opened. Blondie stood in the hall and stared at Jamie. "Your turn."

She glanced at Adam.

His eyes narrowed and he glared over her shoulder. "See you soon, Jamie."

She gulped. She was really doing this. Going somewhere

with an armed man. He could be lying to make it easy to get her where he wanted her. As she approached the door, she saw crooked-nose to the right and a few feet down the hallway, his hand near his holstered gun. Blondie motioned for her to go left. Her shaky legs carried her past three doors on the left before he had her stop at the first door on the right, and pushed it open.

She gave a quick glance down the hall at the other guard, still in position, then up at the one in front of her. He stood a foot taller than her, and probably out-weighed her by a hundred pounds. Theron had said that weight didn't matter. Surprise was more important to take someone down. She knew she could do it, but she'd likely get shot by the other guard. Might as well push a little and hope he didn't take offense. "Why were we kidnapped? Why do we get gym time?"

He stared at her for a few seconds, his mouth a tense line. "You'll find out when it's time why you're here. As far as the gym—" he shrugged— "bosses orders. Workout or take a nap. I'm just supposed to deliver you."

He nodded at the open doorway and she stepped through. The door locked behind her. She did a quick scan of the room. Alone.

A search for cameras found one aimed at the mats in the middle of the room, but more might be hidden. Did they record sparring matches? Or maybe something else happened in this room. She shivered, not wanting to think about it.

Maybe they'd be impressed with how flexible she was in her yoga positions, or that she could run on a treadmill.

The room was maybe twenty feet long and nearly as wide. An exercise bike, a stair stepper, a treadmill, a weight machine, as well as free weights and other equipment she didn't recognize lined the walls. A long punching bag dangled near the weights with gloves on the floor under it.

She had no idea why the kidnapper would let them have exercise time in a gym, but she'd use it to maintain her strength, in case an opportunity presented itself to escape. No way would she reveal her ability to heat by practicing it. If the time was right, it would be ready.

Theron had her lift free weights and kick the punching bag. In her dorm room, she used to do yoga and a few other exercises. She'd start with what she knew. She did her familiar routine, then went on to lifting weights.

Theron. She missed him, and worried about how he was doing. They'd spent nearly every minute of the last month together. Before, during school vacations, she occasionally thought about him, but had never experienced this aching need to be with him. And worry about him.

He'd given up his summer job for her and hadn't been able to keep her safe. It must be tearing him apart. She ached to hold him, to tell him it wasn't his fault.

She pulled in a breath and released it in a rush. She might as well put on the gloves and punch and kick the bag. She probably wasn't the first person to imagine someone's face on the bag as they hit it. She started by imagining it was the gray haired man who killed Walt. He must be the one who had her kidnapped. After she'd given him a few punches and kicks, she imagined the bag was the man who'd given her the injection that had knocked her out and then the man who had held the knife to Abby's throat. If they brought her to the gym again, she'd pretend it was the guards. If a time came when only one guard opened the door, she'd be ready to attack and try to escape. Between Adam and her, they might have a chance to sneak out.

She finished by putting some miles on the treadmill at a slow jog, and was walking to cool down when the door opened.

"Time to go back," Blondie said.

She hadn't noticed when she left her room, but a chair sat on the other side of their door, currently with a guard standing beside it, hand on his gun. Someone must stay near at all times. A paperback book sat on the floor under the chair.

"Hey, could you get us some books? I can't imagine spending the whole day talking to Adam." She froze, expecting a push or gruff answer for her thoughtless question.

"I'll check." He opened the door and she went inside, as he spoke behind her. "Your turn, Adam."

Jamie took a shower and lay down on the bed. Not much else to do. She woke at the sound of keys rattling and the door opening.

Adam walked in with a stack of paperback books in his arms. "One of the guards handed me these." He set them on the table. "I'm going to take a shower."

She stared at the books for a good five minutes. Again she wondered about this imprisonment. Instead of keeping her constantly afraid, or leaving her bored to tears, someone had given her books because she asked for them. Maybe there was something else she could ask for that might actually help them escape.

What was the point of all this? They were treated differently than any kidnap victims she'd heard of.

Jamie hauled herself up to check out the books.

Adam, having finished his shower, stepped beside her and picked one up. "I was surprised when the guard gave me these."

"I asked for books, but I'm surprised too." She picked up *Six Wakes* by Mur Lafferty, flipped it over and read the blurb on the back. A murder mystery in space might be interesting. She set it on her left.

The next book was a graphic sexual novel she'd heard of and never intended to read. "Ugh." She dropped it on the right side of the pile.

Adam picked up the discarded book. "What's wrong with this?"

"I think it's called erotica. I'm not interested."

He flipped it over. "Maybe I'll read it. I might learn a thing or two." He gave her a smile that made her uncomfortable. "Maybe they want us to read it and *do* it."

"Ugh. No. Keep it to yourself." She shivered, and hoped that wasn't the kidnappers' intent. She didn't feel that way about Adam. Especially, now that she had Theron.

She snatched up the next book. *Brainrush* by Richard Bard. The blurb made it sound action packed. Except the part about being kidnapped by a crazy man might be too true to life for her. Theron would love it, and had probably read it already. She sifted through the rest of the books, then moved the two stacks to the dresser, keeping out *Brainrush* to read first. It might help her feel closer to Theron.

Chapter 11

After her workout, Blondie followed Jamie back to the room. Adam passed as she stepped in, his lips pursed, without uttering a word before leaving.

Halfway to the bathroom she paused, taking a sniff. Cologne? Their guards didn't wear any. Did they have a new one?

After her shower, Jamie stepped into the main room. A set of sheets and a stack of towels sat on the bed. She wasn't sure if they'd been there before her shower and she'd simply missed them. Clean bedding after only six days.

She put the towels on a bathroom shelf and hauled out the laundry basket. She and Adam had been placing their used towels and clothes in it, not knowing if someone would take them away to clean. She changed the bed sheets and dropped the dirty ones on the top of the basket and placed it near the door. A laundry service in captivity. She shivered. It meant someone was handling her underwear.

Jamie stared at the bed. After spending one night in a chair, and finding out how extremely uncomfortable it was, she couldn't let Adam sleep in it anymore, so she'd told him they could share the bed. She put a pillow between them each night, but the past three mornings when she woke, Adam's hand rested on her hip or waist. At least the pillow remained between them. The first morning, she felt like a little girl on a playground afraid a boy would give her cooties. It hadn't bothered her as much this morning. He didn't try anything else, and it wasn't like he knew what he did in his sleep.

Adam had been a gentleman on the two dates they'd had. They remained on friendly terms in all the classes they'd shared. She wasn't worried he'd try something, but she'd never expected to find herself sleeping in the same bed with a man who wasn't Theron.

She was lost in her book when the door opened and Adam came in.

"Ten minutes," the guard said before closing the door.

She frowned at Adam. "Ten minutes for what?"

His lips straightened to a line before he spoke. "We have to go upstairs."

"We're finally finding out why we're here!"

"I wouldn't be so excited about it." He grabbed some clothes from the dresser and disappeared into the bathroom.

Her heart thumped loud and fast. She'd almost gotten comfortable. Nothing had happened to scare her since she arrived. Sure, the guards had guns, but they never pulled them out. They hadn't acted threatening. She'd become complacent. If she'd been alone, she'd probably have curled up in a corner, but Adam's calm acceptance kept her sane and toned down her anxiety.

Now fear thrummed as strong as the day she'd been kidnapped. They would find out why they were here, and it wouldn't be good.

Adam came out of the bathroom just as the door opened. Four men stood in the hall. This time, guns were drawn and held at the sides of two of them. Blondie, his gun still in its holster motioned. "You first, Jamie. Follow me," he said as if he were taking her to a dining hall.

He waited until she moved toward him and headed down

the hall, away from the gym. Another man fell in behind her and she glanced over her shoulder, saw he had his gun drawn, his eyes squinting. "No fast moves or you *will* get hurt."

She didn't know if Adam was much of a fighter. All four of the men had guns, and she could only depend on herself to fight them. Theron had taught her a couple of moves to use on one man with one gun, but it was useless with this group. If she tried anything, one of them would tackle her. Probably. She didn't want to think about what a bullet wound would feel like.

Blondie opened a door and they ascended stairs. At the top, a man with a dark beard stood, his hand on his gun. They turned left at the first floor corridor and two more men stepped on each side of her.

Six men with guns. Yeah, they were prepared for whatever scary abilities she or Adam might have. She didn't think these people knew what they were or her fighting skills, but it seemed over the top security.

They turned right and passed several doors, the open ones revealing a couple of rooms with bunk beds, one was a lounge with a talk show on the TV. At the end of the hallway, they turned left.

Glorious sunshine streamed through two full length glass entrance doors. After six days of only fluorescent lights, she wanted to bask in the natural light. A parking lot held several cars, and across the paved street, dense woods might make an excellent escape route, if she didn't get shot in the back first.

She hadn't noticed that she'd slowed until the man behind her told her to keep moving. She'd wanted sunshine for a few moments longer. Trying to escape was pointless.

They stopped at the last door at the end of the hall, and the first man opened the door and proceeded in. She was afraid to enter. The man behind nudged her with his gun. A shiver passed through her. She'd never had a gun pointed at her before. Just a slip of a finger could put a bullet through her.

Blondie pointed to a chair in front of a desk. "Sit there."

Moments later, Adam sat in the chair beside her. Two guards remained at the closed door. She assumed the others waited outside the door. They sat in an office, a dark wood desk in front of them. An open laptop sat in front of the empty chair, with normal office items scattered across the surface.

A gray haired man stood at a window with his back to her. More wonderful sunshine filtered into the room, possibly a northern exposure.

He turned and she gasped. This was the old man who'd killed Walt, and had ordered her kidnapping.

He lifted his eyebrows. "Do you recognize me?"

She shook her head, and stared at the pocket on his shirt instead of looking him in the eye.

He crossed his arms and studied her. She wouldn't give him anything.

He sat behind the desk. "You may call me Connor."

She caught the scent of cologne. The same one she smelled in her room. This man had visited Adam, and Adam hadn't told her. Adam knew what the guard had meant when he'd told him ten minutes. She wondered if Connor had told Adam the purpose of this meeting.

She glanced at Adam, narrowing her eyes, but he stared, expressionless at Connor. They hadn't had a moment to talk, but he could have skipped the shower to tell her about Connor being in their room. Why wouldn't he have taken even a minute to tell her? She didn't want to not trust him.

She lifted her chin.

The old man chuckled. "I like a girl with spunk. How have your accommodations been?"

Seriously? He acted like she was a guest in his house and

not a prisoner locked in a windowless basement room in his compound or whatever this place was. "It would be better if I could leave, if I want."

"All in good time, my girl."

That sounded like he didn't intend to kill her. Or maybe he meant she'd leave dead.

Connor laced his fingers together on the desktop and leaned forward. "Now tell me what abilities you have."

"That's not something I discuss outside my family."

"Consider me family." One corner of his mouth twitched.

Jamie glared. "Yeah. The part of the family no one wants to talk about."

He placed his hands flat on the desk and stood. "I'm going to make an assumption. I believe you can create lightning. Your grandfather, Jonathan Nathaniel Proctor, was quite adept at it."

Dad had told Jason and her that their grandfather had killed her mom's mother and brother by striking a tree with lightning, right after she told him about discovering this new ability. What a way to convince a girl to never want to use it.

"Did you know him?" She wished she could pull the words back. She didn't want to know anything more than she already did about her birth family.

"Oh, yes. He was a remarkable man, as was his son."

Her birth father. The killer. Not at all surprising that a killer appreciated another killer. "How did you know I was related to the Proctors?"

"Nathan Proctor was a close friend and business associate. I saw you on the day you were born."

Her breath caught in her throat and she suppressed a shiver. This evil man had touched her life from the beginning. Did he kidnap her because he suspected she could create lightning or because he felt they were connected?

"Now, go to that window." Connor tipped his head

96

toward it.

She glared at him. He couldn't think it would be that easy to make her do what he wanted.

"Now!"

The new guard, who had walked behind her, stepped up and rested his hand on his gun.

It was hard to be defiant with guns around. This was a test of some kind, and she wished she had the courage to fail it. On shaky legs, she stood as slowly as she thought he'd allow, and made her way to the window. She'd wanted to feel the sunshine, but right now, she'd rather be back in her windowless prison.

A quick glance outside showed her a big field with a lone tree near the edge of woods. She turned to face Connor.

He pointed at a spot near the edge of the window. "Adam. Stand there."

Adam joined them, the bearded guard at his side.

Connor pointed at the lone tree. "Now, my dear, strike the tree with lightning."

She glared into his eyes. "No." She should have said she couldn't do it. Now, he'd know she could and refused.

Connor tipped his head and the guard jabbed Adam in the stomach with his fist. Adam grunted and doubled over.

Jamie flinched. She'd caused his pain. Her heart pounded, but she tried to keep her breathing even. If she did what Connor wanted, he'd probably push for her to do more. If she didn't, Adam would be beaten.

She hated being in this position. She wanted to be home with Theron, and catching up with her family. But this man enjoyed forcing people to do what he wanted, and didn't care how he did it.

Adam was slow to straighten. His eyes glistened.

"Jamie, I'm all right." The pain in his eyes contradicted the words.

She glared at the guard as he kept his hand fisted, ready for the order to strike again.

"I'm sure Art will enjoy every punch he gives Adam. Make your choice."

She stared at Adam, and he kept his head turned to the scene outside the window. He would let Art beat him senseless if she couldn't bring herself to perform for Connor. She wouldn't let that happen. Seeing his pain once was enough. Besides, Connor already knew she could create lightning. It was only a tree.

She sighed and turned back to the window. Squinting at the tree, she judged its distance, then held up her hand, fingers spread, drawing in energy. It felt like a lifetime ago she'd done this last, but it wasn't something she'd forget how to do. Then she snapped her hand toward the tree, releasing her energy. Lightning arced out of the cloudless sky to the tree. The crack of thunder pounded in her ears, sparks flew out from the strike, and fire leaped into the air.

"Excellent!" Connor continued to stare out the window.

She grabbed the window sill, staggered by the energy loss. Most of it was the energy she'd gathered for the blast, but some of her own strength had gone with it.

A black SUV drove to the tree. Two men got out and used fire extinguishers on the tree trunk. She didn't know why they would. It wasn't enough to put out the fire, and with no wind, it wasn't likely to spread to the forest. One man ran to the car and pulled a stretcher from the back and returned to the tree. Together, they lifted a body and placed it on the stretcher, carrying it to the vehicle.

Had Connor tied someone to the tree so that she'd kill him? She wavered between horror and anger. She would not intentionally take a life. That was the key. Intentionally. This wasn't her fault. It was a setup by Connor.

The SUV drove up to the window. The men retrieved the

stretcher and carried it to the window. Jamie didn't want to look at a burnt body, but her eyes dropped to the sight. Walt. Because of the burns, she couldn't be a hundred-percent sure, but the cut on the throat convinced her.

Connor chuckled. "Oh, dear. Look what you've done, Jamie. He must have taken refuge in the shade, and you killed him."

He wanted to make her feel guilty, and for a few moments she had. Did he think that if she thought she'd killed one man accidentally, it would be easier to kill another on purpose? She'd hated having the premonition dream, but now was glad. The relief of knowing she hadn't killed Walt far outweighed the horror of seeing his blood spill in a premonition.

She glared at him, but said nothing. Let him think what he wants.

He stared out the window. "How far is your reach?"

"I have no idea. I don't practice it, and I don't intend to." She lifted her chin. A few times after she made her first accidental lightning strike, she'd created lightning during rain storms, figuring no one would know it wasn't natural. Each time, her second strike was weaker than the first, and the third was barely visible. She'd been exhausted, and had to hide the reason from her family.

Then her mother invited a family to stay on the third floor while repairs were done on their home that had been badly damaged by a lightning strike. Her lightning strike. They could have died. She'd never done it again.

"We shall see, my dear. We shall see."

The same guards walked them back to their room. She was relieved to be away from Connor. The man exuded evil. She hadn't picked up on that in the premonition, except for the creepy smile when he killed Walt.

As soon as the door closed behind them, she spun to face

Adam, hands on her hips. "Connor was in here while I was in the gym. I could smell his aftershave. What did he want?"

Adam ran his hands through his hair. "He—wanted to tell me how today would go."

She flung her hands up. "Why bother?" She pointed at the ceiling. "It didn't influence what happened up there. What else did he want?"

He walked past her. "I don't want to talk about it." He lay on the bed and dropped his arm over his eyes.

Hands back on hips, Jamie glared at him. Not that it was satisfying since he couldn't see it. Connor wouldn't come down to only tell Adam that he'd force Jamie into a lightning demonstration. She wracked her brain and couldn't come up with anything else Connor would have thought important enough to visit Adam.

***

Theron stumbled into the kitchen, grabbed a cup from the cabinet and poured coffee. He sat at the bar and ran a hand down his face. He'd had a dream of making love to Jamie, which made his heart ache more.

No sign had turned up. She'd disappeared without a trace. He might never see his wonderful Jamie again. He couldn't live with that. She couldn't be one of the hundreds of people who disappeared and are never heard from again. He closed his eyes and rubbed his chest, waiting for the raw pain to pass.

Jason stood at the sliding glass doors with his back to the room, his phone to his ear, and his voice an indecipherable mumble. He dropped his hand, turned around, and pumped his fist in the air. "Yes!"

Theron straightened, hopeful for the first time in eight days. "What is it?"

Jason grinned. "Walt's body turned up."

Theron nearly upended his chair pushing it back to stand. "Where? Let's go."

Jason held up his hand. "Hold on. He was in the Charles River. Got hung up at Charles River Park in Needham. It looks like his body was in the river a few days."

Theron fisted his hands. "But we could still go there—"

"And what? There won't be evidence where the body washed up. It could have floated miles down the river, and the killer could have driven from any direction to dump him. Mark will send the autopsy report, but I don't think it will help us. What we've learned is that Jamie is likely in eastern Massachusetts. So, she's not across the country. And Walt's throat was cut, just like in Jamie's premonition, so likely, that also means they don't intend to kill her."

Theron slumped back into his chair. Good, but not good enough. He needed to get out there and do more to find her, but the only thing he could do was keep in shape and not fall apart.

He had to get outside. Fresh air and more practice. Once in the center of the yard, he didn't want to go through his stretches. He needed action.

A survey of the yard found many dead branches high in the trees. He could take care of that.

He picked a bare limb in a maple tree, and thrust his arm out, palm facing the tree. He concentrated his energy and pushed it through with a burst. The limb cracked and swayed, but didn't break.

The two previous real life uses of this ability were when he'd been attacked late at night, in places he shouldn't have been. Close up, he didn't need to put as much energy into punches, and he hadn't wanted to kill them. What he'd done to the tree would have been a kill shot on a man. Exactly what he wanted to do to the man responsible for kidnapping

Jamie.

He struck the limb again with more energy. It cracked and fell, hitting a lower branch before rolling off and landing with a reverberating thump on the ground. One down.

He brought down seven more branches before he tired, then dragged his mess to the pile of branches in the far corner of the yard, and headed back towards the house.

Jason leaned against the open door. "Hey, thanks. Now I won't have to hire a tree service to take those down."

Theron shrugged. "Guess I'm earning my room and board." He glanced at the fence and up at the treetops. "Oh, man. Your neighbors—"

"Saw worse before I moved here. It probably won't faze them."

Theron felt ready for anything. Now he needed a target.

Chapter 12

Eleven days. Jamie had carefully kept track of how long she'd been held. It felt like forever. Theron was looking for her, and with her family's help, they *would* find her. Before it was too late. She hoped.

She lay flat on her back on a mat in the gym after working especially hard, trying to make sure she stayed in shape to improve her chances of escaping. Usually, she worked until the guard came to get her, but today, exhaustion had claimed her first. Her legs barely carried her to the mat, and maybe they'd turned on the heat because her whole body felt overheated. She touched the back of her hand to her forehead. No fever.

The lock turned and she scrambled to her feet, not wanting to be seen as weak. She paused a second to catch her balance before joining Blondie in the corridor. The window in the door across from her caught her eye. Every day since coming to the gym, it had been dark, but today, a light shone in the window.

Curiosity nipped at her, so she hurried across the hall and peeked into the small window. It contained a couch instead of two chairs, but other than that, the furnishings were the same.

"Get moving." He pushed the middle of her back.

She made a quick inspection of the next two rooms,

which were also lit for the first time. One held a couch and the other contained two chairs like her room. With three other rooms or more with beds to choose from, why had she and Adam been put together? Were they easier to keep track of?

Adam brushed past her without a word as she arrived back in their room. They'd have to talk about it when he returned.

She stared at the closed door. Adam had seemed…angry? She surveyed the room. Everything appeared normal. A sniff didn't detect any unusual scents.

Maybe he'd had a visitor, like the day they'd been brought to Connor. Her heart skipped a beat then sped up. She didn't want the same thing as last time to happen again, but if they came for her, she wouldn't have a choice.

She cooled off in the shower, massaging her sore muscles, and reviewed what she'd say to Adam.

Adam returned and she pounced on him after his shower. "We need to talk."

He sat in the upholstered chair next to hers. A wrinkle creased the space between his brows. "You seem anxious. Did something happen with the guards?"

She leaned towards him. "You tell me. You seemed angry when you left. Who was in here?"

He rubbed his forehead, and glanced at her then away. "That guard from upstairs who hit me. He came in and taunted me."

She sucked in a breath. "Did he hurt you?"

He shook his head. "He didn't touch me."

Thank God. She leaned back. "What did he want?"

His lips pressed together. "To aggravate me. I don't want to talk about it." He stood.

"Wait." Jamie reached out, but didn't touch him. "There's something else."

He let out a long breath and returned to his seat.

She pointed in the direction of the rooms she'd seen. "Today, the lights were on in those rooms. There are beds in all of them. All this time, I thought this was the only bed and that's why they stuck us together. Why didn't they put us in separate rooms?"

Adam didn't immediately answer, as if he was shifting gears from the other discussion. "Maybe they thought you'd be more comfortable if you weren't alone." A hint of a smile flicked across his lips. "You've been a much needed calming influence on me. I hope I've helped you, too."

"I'm sure it's easier with you here. But two of those rooms had couches. One of us could have slept on it."

Adam stared at the floor. "Maybe they want us to share a bed."

Panic welled up. Maybe Connor had told him to have sex with her. The guard might have been taunting him for not having done it yet. She shuddered to think how they'd know it hadn't happened, and pushed it away. "You mean, because we might have sex? Why?"

He shrugged, but didn't look at her. "Or, at least, become closer."

She and Adam *had* become closer, but not in that way. No one was a better champ than her at keeping guys in the friend zone. She loved Theron, and the thought of sex with anyone else was revolting.

He took a deep breath, let it out slowly, and looked at her. "Jamie, it's only a guess. Mostly, I think it's so we keep each other sane."

She deflated against the chair back. Sane. Connor wouldn't care if they were sane as long as he got what he wanted. Sometimes, she felt half insane from worry over what would be expected of her next. "Nothing's happened since the lightning day. Every morning, I wonder if it'll be the day they come back for us again."

He patted her hand. "In their own time. And I'm sure, whatever it is, we won't like it."

"Maybe Theron and Jason will find us before then." She hoped it wouldn't be impossible.

Adam's eyebrows rose. "Who are they?"

"Theron's my boyfriend. Jason's my brother."

He squinted. "Theron? That name sounds familiar. I didn't think you had a boyfriend."

She smiled. "Theron Jarvis. He's been my friend for ages. Now he's my boyfriend." Her gut twisted. They'd spent so little time together as a couple. "If we ever get out of here."

***

Two days later, Jamie and Adam were marched into Connor's office with full complement of guards. The guards pushed them into chairs in front of Connor's desk.

Connor gave her a sickening smile. "Jamie. I have a chore for you."

She crossed her arms and lifted her chin. "I'm not doing anything for you."

"Don't be that way. You haven't heard what I want or what will happen if you refuse."

She glared at him. She hated this man who could murder without a qualm.

He leaned forward. "There's a power station that I want you to destroy with lightning."

"Why?" She shouldn't have responded.

"You don't need to know that. But, I will tell you that this is an unmanned station, so have no fear that you'll kill someone."

That did help, if he was telling the truth, but she didn't want to blow up something that cost tens of thousands of dollars. And whatever the reason, it was so Connor could do

106

something bad.

She clenched her hands her in lap. "Is this the reason you brought me here?"

Connor leaned back in his chair and crossed his arms over his chest. "One of several. You'll learn about them as needed."

That sounded like he planned on keeping her forever. She hated doing what he wanted.

He leaned forward, placing his hands flat on the desk. "Now, the lightning—"

"I've never created lightning where I couldn't see what I wanted to strike." Hopefully, he understood that it was impossible. Or, better yet, he'd take her to the site and she could try to escape.

"Your grandfather didn't have to be there. You don't, either. I'll give you the coordinates."

She pushed her hands into the sides of the chair. "Coordinates? I'm not a GPS."

Connor squinted at her. "You'll figure it out, or"—his eyes flicked to Adam—"Adam suffers. And Art would enjoy hitting him again."

She studied Adam. He held her attention, showing no fear, and didn't beg her to do it. His bravery in letting her make the decision, knowing he could be injured, decided her. Maybe that was why he'd been kidnapped. So they'd have a way to make her do what they wanted.

She sighed and turned back to Connor. There was only one way to prevent Adam from being injured. "I'll need to see a map that shows where I am in relation to this power station. I can't guarantee I'll hit it. I've never done this before."

"I knew you'd agree. Give me a minute." He pulled the laptop in front of him and tapped on the keys. A few minutes later, he turned it to face her.

A Google map showed two points with a line between. Seventeen-point-four miles separated them, if it was driven. Direct, it would be shorter. It scared her that she might miss and strike a house or a school. She stared intently at the map, particularly concentrating on the marker for the power station. The topographical map showed no schools near the station. A chain link fence enclosed the station, but two homes sat across the street and down a bit. At this distance, she could easily miss the station and hit one of those houses. And if someone was home…She didn't want to think about it.

This station had to be a big deal. It sent electricity to something Connor was interested in. It could be big for her, too. A huge power outage might draw some attention. And caused by a lightning strike out of a clear blue sky had to make Theron sit up and take notice. It could reassure him that she was still alive, and maybe narrow down the search area.

She lifted her shaky hand, fingers straight. She strengthened her resolve before pulling in energy, or she might hit something other than the target. And she still might miss, never having done this before. She sensed she needed extra power this time, since she would be directing it from farther away, and drew in more than she'd ever held before. When the energy had built sufficiently, she curled her fingers and snapped them open again, never taking her eyes from the target on the map.

She exhaled and sagged against the back of the chair, glad she'd been seated. "It's done."

The only sound in the room was the hum of the fan on the laptop. Connor stared at her and she glared back. The room lights flickered, but remained lit.

The desk phone rang and Connor picked it up. "Is it destroyed?"

A voice mumbled from the receiver. "Good." Connor

hung up. "You were successful." He glanced behind her. "Take them back to their room."

***

Theron ran another lap around the park and headed back to Jason's house. Jason had spent a good deal of the last few days at his office in Amherst. It was like everything had gotten back to normal. It wasn't normal, not until Jamie was back home. It felt like everyone had given up. Except him. He couldn't give up, but frustration had escalated at his inability to rescue her.

He ran up the steps and into the house, heading straight for the shower. Afterward, he entered the kitchen and found Jason nursing a cup of coffee while he read through some papers.

Theron poured himself coffee. "Do you want to spar?"

"No. The last time we sparred, you nearly killed me."

"I need to stay in shape to rescue Jamie." He didn't know what they'd face when they found her, but he had to make sure he could get her out.

"I've fought with the best, but you're over-the-top too intense. Why don't I take you to the dojo and you can pick the toughest looking guy and spar with him?"

"Fine, since you're so soft."

A short drive later, they walked through the doors of *Shotokan Studio*, each carrying a bag, and Theron scanned the large room. It was very much like the one he used at home. On one side of the room, a class was in progress with mostly teens. The other side of the room had two sparring areas, one in use. Theron guessed they were inexperienced since they took hesitant swipes at each other.

Jason headed to the back. "Let's see what Joe has to say."

Inside an office, a man sat at a desk, pecking with two

fingers on a keyboard. Jason tapped once on the doorframe, and the man looked up and smiled. "Jason. What's it been? A year?"

Jason smiled and entered the room, holding out his hand. "About that. I'm back for good now."

The older man took his hand, and looked at Theron. "And who's your friend?"

"Joe, this is Theron. He's a little too intense for me. Do you have anyone he can expend some energy on?"

Joe's eyebrows rose. "There's someone you can't whip?" He dropped his hands on his hips and lowered his head. After a few seconds, it popped back up. "There's a new guy who's been coming the last few months. He's been holding his own. I think I heard his voice a bit ago."

Joe led them out of the office, stopped and searched around, then proceeded to a man punching a bag. He paused in the man's line of sight and waited.

After a few more punches, the man dropped his hands and turned. "What's up, Joe?"

He motioned to Theron. "Eric, I got a guy who wants to spar with you."

Eric looked Theron up and down. "How good are you?"

"I can take anything you dish out and do you one better." He'd been in plenty of competitions and scored well.

Eric smirked. "Sure, ya can." His confident stance and bulging muscles push Theron to trust the man's assessment.

Theron swung his bag. "Let me gear up and I'll be right out."

Nervous energy ran through Theron's muscles. He hoped Eric was good. Otherwise, the guy might wind up seriously hurt.

Theron could usually temper his strength, but with Jamie missing, anger and worry simmered just below the surface, needing an outlet. Once he started sparring, his thoughts always turned to Jamie and the need to be ready when they found her. His opponent, Jason thus far, became the enemy.

He returned to the floor to find Joe still talking to Jason and Eric. With two of them watching, they'd stop him if he got out of hand.

He stepped into position on the mat and Eric followed. They raised their gloved hands, staring each other down, and waited for the signal.

"Start," Joe called out.

They bounced back and forth, each taking an occasional jab, watching how the other reacted. Theron lunged, sweeping out a leg and took out one of Eric's, making him stumble. Eric rolled and caught Theron with a side kick to the ribs as he righted himself. They circled again.

Instinct took over. Theron could do this in his sleep. All thoughts were pushed aside as he countered kicks and punches and snuck in his own when openings presented. The longer they sparred, the more weaknesses he found in his opponent. He'd take advantage of one, but before long, Eric realized his error and corrected. Theron took advantage of another, then another.

A whistle blew and they froze. Theron stepped back and scanned the room. A crowd surrounded their mat. The teens from the class he'd seen earlier, and others who had been working out, had gathered to watch the two spar. Cheers and clapping erupted.

Theron was used to practicing in the studio at home or near campus, or going to competitions with a lot of other good athletes. He was taken by surprise with the reaction of these people.

Joe stepped up to them and clapped a hand on each of their shoulders. "I don't think I've ever seen two men so closely matched. I could have watched all day, but I let it go on too long as it was. Great job."

Theron shook Eric's hand. "Thanks. I really needed that."

"Me, too, man. I usually have to hold back. I haven't been able to fight like that since I left my unit. Any time you want a rematch let me know. Joe's got my number." He headed to the locker room.

The crowd dispersed.

Jason grinned. "Wow, Theron. I had no idea. I mean, I knew you were better than me, but that was amazing."

"Thanks for bringing me here. I'll be as quick as I can." He took off for the locker room.

Back in the car later, a news report caught Theron's attention. "Needham, Newton, West Roxbury, and Dedham are without power due to a freak lightning strike to a power station. Power is being rerouted and should be restored to most customers in the next twenty-four hours. Those closest to the station may be without power for up to three days as repairs are made to the station."

Cold enveloped Theron. "That had to be Jamie."

Jason glanced at him, eyes widened. "You know she can create lightning?"

"Yes. Skies are clear, so that wasn't a natural lightning strike."

Jason's expression darkened. "I know. It must have been her. Walt's body was found in that area, too."

Jamie wouldn't have done it unless she was forced to. Fear gripped Theron with thoughts of what they could have done to get her to comply.

"It's time to go find Jamie!"

Jason huffed out a long breath. "They could have brought her to that power station and be miles away now. How do you propose we search for her?"

"You're the expert," Theron yelled. "Why can't *you* figure that out? Can't your mom do something?"

Jason pulled into his driveway and tapped his fingers on

the steering wheel. "Mom's mind reading only reaches about a mile away. And if she doesn't have a specific target location, she has to expend more energy to disperse it. I don't know how long she'll last doing it."

"So far, we're doing nothing. Isn't it worth a try? If you don't ask her, I will." He glared at Jason.

"All right. I'll call her." He got out of the car and pulled his phone from his pocket.

***

Theron examined the remains of the burnt out power station as Jason pulled to the curb across the street from it. The gigantic power box could have been bombed with the way the top half had been torn off. Several power lines dangled inside the chain link fence. Two utility trucks sat next to the open gate and a flatbed truck backed into the space. A crane poised over the mess as four men power wrenched fist-sized bolts from the base.

Jason's voice brought Theron's attention back to the inside of the SUV. "Can you get anything, Mom?"

Her eyes were closed and a crease furrowed the space between her brows. She sighed and slumped against the seat. "Nothing."

They'd left home at six that morning and it was just after eight.

Jason pulled away from the curb. "Okay. Let's move out."

Theron had sat mostly silent in the backseat as Jason and Kathleen discussed the strategy of their hunt. Initially, she'd wanted to keep broadcasting once they reached the power station, but Jason thought she'd tire too quickly. His plan was to stop every one-and-three-quarter miles for her to try again. Her outreach would overlap slightly, cover the same area as a continuous broadcast, and give her recovery time between stops.

They headed towards the location where Walt's body was found and would continue to follow the river up stream. Jason had found an estimate on how fast something would float on the Charles River, and mapped the length of their route accordingly. Once they reached the limit, he'd head a mile-and-a-half perpendicular, and parallel the first route. And repeat.

Theron stopped counting after Kathleen made the twentieth attempt to reach Jamie. His stomach rumbled, but he wouldn't be the one to request a lunch break. Maybe he would. Kathleen looked worn out, as if she'd been awake for three days straight.

Jason touched the screen on his phone. "All right. Let's take a lunch break." He glanced at his mother. "Why don't you tip your seat back and rest until we get there?"

"I'm not going to fall asleep."

Jason touched her arm. "I know, Mom. But you'll recover faster if you relax."

"All right." She tipped the seat back and closed her eyes. Ten minutes later, her eyes popped open when Jason put the car in park and turned it off. They faced a *Burger King*.

They made quick work of a meal, then Jason drove to the next location. The afternoon progressed the same as the morning as they worked their way west from the power station.

They ate dinner at a family style restaurant and headed out for a couple more hours.

At the last stop, Jason ran a hand through his hair. "Okay, Mom. That's it for today."

"Jason, I can go a little longer."

"No, Mom. You're exhausted."

Theron had to agree. He'd love to continue, but Kathleen

looked ready to drop.

Jason put the car in drive. "We'll pick up in the morning. Head farther south and then a little on the other side of the Charles."

They found a motel and checked in. Kathleen in one room, and Jason and Theron sharing the one beside it.

Before she entered her room, Theron hugged her. "Thank you for doing this."

Even worn out, there was a determined gleam in her eyes. "I have to do this for my daughter."

"I know. But thanks, anyway."

***

After breakfast at a café, they worked a grid south of the one from the day before. Theron's frustration mounted. He'd been sure that by the end of the first day, they would have gotten a lock on Jamie. Nothing.

During lunch, Jason mapped out their grid for the other side of the river and they headed over a bridge after eating. It was another fruitless search.

At four o'clock Jason pushed back in his seat. "We're done."

Theron leaned forward. "We can't be. Jamie could be two miles from here."

"Or she could be twenty!" Jason took his mother's hand. "Theron, look at her. She can't do anymore."

Her face was more haggard than the end of the day before. She'd tried her best. If Jamie would have been in the many square miles they'd covered, she would have found her.

He'd been so hopeful when they'd started out, so sure they'd find her. Now, he felt farther from Jamie than ever. Would he ever see her again?

Chapter 13

Twenty days. Jamie never expected it to take this long for Theron and Jason to find her. Maybe they never would. How long would she stay in this holding pattern? Day after day. Meals and gym, and an occasional book exchange. A couple of days before, a stack of new, untouched books had been given to her. She must have run through all the books they had on hand.

Fear had subsided to only the times something was different, like being taken to Connor, or when she and Adam guessed at the reasons they were there.

The door opened, and Blondie stuck his head in. "Jamie, gym time."

She sighed and preceded him to the gym. Lethargy had settled in, a sign of depression. Her chest ached with thoughts of Theron and her family, and each day that passed increased the likelihood that she'd never see them again.

She vowed that in another twenty days, if she was still alive and hadn't been rescued, she would strike lightning to the building, centered on Connor's office. If the building caught on fire, would they open the door and take her out, giving her a chance to escape into the woods? But if they left her locked inside, she'd be dead and Connor's evil plans would end. She wouldn't be forced to hurt or kill people.

Except, if she did strike the building, she'd be the one deciding to kill.

Having a vague plan that gave her some control over her life made her feel a bit better. The only ones her life or death mattered to were Theron and her family who would mourn her, never knowing for sure if she was alive or dead.

Most days lately, she'd picked at her food, not feeling hungry enough to use the energy to chew. The only reason she'd eaten as much as she had was because Adam encouraged and prodded her.

She started with stretches, then moved onto the stair stepper, and worked her way through her normal routine. She'd done fewer reps at each station, tiring faster than usual. From what she remembered, exhaustion was another sign of depression.

With fifteen minutes left of her gym time, she sat cross-legged on a mat, out of sight of the camera, closed her eyes and thought of Theron. She'd known him for three years. They'd met at a party, the first one she'd attended sophomore year. They'd each been brought by a girlfriend. At one point, they'd ended up seated near each other and chatted for a few minutes. They frequently attended games with the same friends or went out as a group on weekends.

This past year, he'd invited her to movies or out to eat. It had never felt like a date because he'd become her closest friend. She wished she'd seen it sooner. It took a dream to wake up her true feelings for him, the same feelings he had for her for who-knew-how-long.

They'd been together for barely a month as a couple. She hoped that wasn't all the time they'd have.

The keys rattled in the lock, and she scrambled to her feet, not wanting anyone to know how badly this imprisonment affected her. What would Connor do if he saw her as weak? Kill her? Take advantage?

***

Crooked-nose brought in their lunch, set it on the table, and picked up the breakfast tray. "You've got an hour."

She snapped her head up. "For what?"

He left without answering.

She sat in front of a plate and lifted the cover. A ham sandwich and potato salad.

Adam joined her, uncovering his own food.

She glanced at him. "What do you think happens in an hour?"

He shook his head. "We're going upstairs again, but I don't know why. Maybe Connor wants to find out what other abilities you have."

It was bad enough he knew she could create lightning, what would he do if he discovered her other secrets? "Why isn't he trying to find your abilities?"

Adam stared at his plate. "I don't think I'm the important one here. You're strong. You sent lightning seventeen miles away." He waved his hand. "You've got that hot hand thing."

She leaned forward and whispered. "You haven't told anyone have you?"

He frowned. "Jamie, why would I tell them? They'd find a way to use it against you."

There had to be a reason why Connor kidnapped Adam. They just didn't know yet Connor's plan for him.

Too soon, the door opened again, and a group of guards stood in the corridor. "Time to go."

Her stomach heaved and she took deep breaths to calm it. Her body had turned to jelly, not wanting to follow them.

Connor hadn't hurt her the other two times he'd summoned them, but that didn't mean he wouldn't. He'd tried to trick her into thinking she'd killed a man. He might try to force her to do it knowingly. Not for the first time, she wished she didn't have her abilities. Why couldn't she have something totally defensive, like her mom's protective bubbles, or fun, like reading a history of objects? Adam squeezed her shoulder, waiting for her to rise.

She stood, chin held high, and stepped into the hallway, a guard slid in between her and Adam.

Whatever Connor wanted, she'd find a way through. And if he told her to kill, she'd call down lightning on him, likely killing everyone in the room, including her.

At the top of the stairs, they took a different route, ending at the back of the building in a huge empty room with a carpeted floor. Straight across from the door, was another door. Several windows lined the same wall. Unfortunately, it was an overcast day. Connor stood near the door, and four guards remained with them when the doors closed.

Connor stared at her. "Thank you for joining me."

Like she had a choice. She folded her arms across her chest.

He smiled. "I have a little competition for you." He pointed to the door across the room. "If you can get through that door, you're free to leave."

Jamie glanced at the door and back to Connor. "What's the catch?"

He squinted and his smile turned sinister. He raised his voice. "Let them in."

Six men came through a door on the left. They wore various shades of blue jeans. Four wore t-shirts and two were in tank shirts. They positioned themselves in twos between her and the door. Two with broad shoulders and bulked up arms stood closest to her target door. Another broad man stood in the center, near a tall, thin man with a tremor in his hands. The closest two, although not as big as the bulky men, looked the meanest, one with a long scar on his cheek. None had weapons in their hands, but that didn't make it a fair

119

fight.

All stared intently at her, with their arms slightly away from their sides. She'd only fought Theron. Sure, he'd gotten more aggressive as her skills advanced, but that couldn't prepare her for six men.

"They've been told to prevent you from reaching the door, or they die. Quite the incentive, don't you think?"

She clutched her throat. "If I win, they die?"

He shrugged. "Maybe, maybe not."

He was capable of it. Would he kill all these men for one thing done wrong?

She sucked in a breath. "If I make it through the door, Adam comes with me." These men volunteered for whatever this was, she and Adam hadn't. Or maybe they didn't volunteer. She glanced at the skinny man with the trembling hands. They could be trapped in this as much as she was.

Connor's eyes flicked to Adam and back to her. "Yes, of course."

Adam grabbed her arm. "Jamie, you don't have to do this." The distress in his voice pulled at her.

She turned back to Connor. "And if I refuse?"

He nodded to the center of the room. "Then those six men will be allowed to do whatever they want to Adam."

She didn't know how well Adam fought, but she figured they'd converge on him all at once, especially if the guards held him until the other men got to him. Would they kill him or be called off before that?

She glared at Connor. She didn't trust him, but it was the first chance she'd gotten. Guards with guns could be on the other side of that door to bring her back, but there was no choice, anyway. She'd need to use her heat ability, giving Connor another skill to use. "All right. I'll do it."

"Jamie, no!" Adam lunged, but two guards struggled, holding him back.

"Start when you're ready, my dear."

With her heart beating like pistons, she burst to the side, hoping to catch the men by surprise. The closest one reached her, and she skidded onto her side, swiping her legs across, knocking him off his feet. She sprang up, and kicked the next man in the crotch. He doubled over as she moved on to her third opponent.

Energy coursed through her. She felt like she could fly.

The thin man reached out to grab her, but she yanked his arm and tossed him over her hip, landing him on the first man, who had started to rise.

She went to kick the fourth man in the crotch, but he caught her foot. A moment of panic seized her, but Theron's training kicked in again. She twisted out of his grasp, swung around and smashed his nose with her palm before elbowing him under the chin.

The last two guys came at her side-by-side. Her heart stopped then kicked into overdrive. She didn't have a choice this time. She couldn't take on both at once with her fighting skills. Just as they reached her, she grabbed their necks and turned up the heat on her hands. She made them hotter than she'd ever done before. Strangled screams were all they seemed to manage. They slipped from her hands, falling to the floor.

"Jamie! Behind you!"

With Adam's yell, she leaped to the side and turned, her breath coming in short gasps. A man barreled toward where she would have been without the warning, but now he passed on her left. She grabbed his arm as he reached for her, ducking under. Pulled off balance, he stumbled. She twisted his arm behind him and drove him to the floor, smacking his head with her palm so that it bounced on the floor.

Jamie jumped up and away from him. He didn't rise. She backed up toward the door, eyeing the downed men. Finally, her back hit the door and she quickly turned, grabbed the knob and turned it, but the door wouldn't budge.

"No!" With frustration, she took a step back and kicked next to the knob over and over, with no effect.

"Jamie!" Connor's firm voice grated.

She turned and glared at him.

"I forgot to tell you something, my dear."

She wanted to wipe that smirk off his face, wipe out his whole body. Too bad she couldn't shoot the heat out of her hands.

"There's a bar across the outside of the door. You'll have to try harder than that to open it."

She slid down the door in a heap on the floor, exhausted. It wasn't a surprise that he'd made sure she couldn't escape. He'd wanted to trick her into revealing more abilities, and it had worked spectacularly. That tiny flicker of hope died.

Connor waved toward the men scattered on the floor. "Kill them."

Jamie lifted her head. "No. I didn't make it out."

"Their task was to prevent you from getting *to* the door. They failed."

Two guards moved forward, each heading to a different man, knives in hand. They cut the throats of the unconscious men. Then moved onto the next.

One guard straightened. "This one's dead already." One of the men she'd burned. Chilled fingers ran down her spine.

As he moved on to his third man, the other guard reached his last. "This one's dead, too." He smiled at Jamie and gave her a thumbs up. She buried her head in her arms. She'd killed. These men had been fighting for their lives. All were dead because of her. She so wanted to believe she could escape.

A hand touched her shoulder and she jumped, not having the strength to fight. She looked into Adam's compassionate face. "Come on, Jamie. Let's go back to our room."

She swiped at the tears on her cheeks and nodded. With Adam's help, she stumbled to her feet.

They reached the door to the corridor and Connor touched her arm. She jerked away.

"I'm quite impressed with your fighting skills, and your ability."

She glared. "When is this going to be over?"

His lips firmed and he squinted. "When I say it is." He nodded at the guards. "Take them."

With guards in front and behind, keeping a greater distance than before, they returned to the room she'd grown used to. She kicked off her shoes, headed to the bed, and curled up under the covers. Adrenalin, stress and then defeat had taken its toll.

Adam curled up behind her and kissed the crown of her head. "I'm sorry, Jamie. I wish there was something I could do."

Nobody could do anything. Her life was in Connor's hands. She was like a puppet, and Adam was the strings, and Connor the puppet master.

At this point, she didn't care that no pillow separated her from Adam. She needed to draw on his warmth and comfort.

***

Theron had sparred with Eric that morning, so he'd grabbed a fast food lunch to eat back at the house. He was almost finished, when fear struck. He gasped, grabbed his chest and closed his eyes.

He couldn't see, didn't know what was happening, but Jamie's emotions flooded through him. Fear, and then an adrenalin rush, and near panic. She was fighting. His Jamie, who he should be protecting, had to fight for her life. The pain of his helplessness tore through him. He pushed his strength out, hoping to feed it to her. He didn't know if it worked or if it made a difference.

He tried to tune in more, to understand, to see what she saw. Raw emotion boiled over him, nothing more. And then it was over. Heartache hit him. She was alive, but something bad had happened. He felt her defeat. He couldn't imagine what she'd gone through. What she'd been forced to do, or what had been forced on her.

She needed to be rescued. *Jamie, hang on. We're going to find you.*

He came back to himself to find Jason shaking his shoulders. "Theron! Come out of it! Theron!"

Theron raised his arms. "Okay, okay. I'm back." He felt wetness on his cheeks and swiped them. Were these Jamie's tears?

Jason collapsed in the chair beside him. "What was that? I heard you scream, and found you thrashing in your chair."

"I'm not sure. It's never happened before. I think Jamie fought in some kind of battle. And then she felt defeated." He wiped his cheeks again.

"Wow. I didn't know you could do that."

Theron shook his head. "I could only feel she was alive before. This was the first I felt anything else."

Theron slammed his fist on the counter. "We've got to find her."

"I know, and we will as soon as we've got something worth checking. I've got Mark looking for anything unusual in the area between the body and the lighting strike."

He raised his hands and yelled. "That's all you keep saying and we've gotten almost nowhere. We need to go look."

Jason squeezed Theron's shoulder. "I know how you feel, but—"

"Do you?" He shrugged off Jason's hand and glared. He started quiet, but his voice rose with each word. "You knew who kidnapped Shauna. You knew where they were going. You got her back in five hours." His pain ramped up, and he stood. "We don't know who took Jamie or where they have her, or why they took her. She's been missing for three weeks. You don't know how I feel."

Jason grabbed his arm. "She's my sister and I love her. I know how you feel."

Theron dropped his shoulders and tipped his head back, gulping in air, trying to corral his rage and helplessness. "Sorry. Every day that passes that we don't learn anything new gets harder. I need to get out there and *do* something."

Chapter 14

Jamie sat on the bathroom floor with her head and back against the wall, letting the tile cool her heated body. Awakened with the urge to throw up in the middle of the night wasn't high on her list of new experiences.

Water ran and she cracked her eyes open. Adam squeezed out a washcloth and sat beside her. He patted her face with it, cooling her overheated skin.

"Are you okay? What happened?"

His concern made her eyes burn. She was probably the reason he was stuck here, but he still treated her as a good friend. She rocked her head from side to side. "I keep having flashes of those men I burned." She grabbed his hand. "I killed people." She closed her eyes and tipped her head back. Tears leaked from between her lids.

Adam gently wiped them away. "Jamie, it wasn't your fault. You were forced into that. If you hadn't killed them, they would still be dead like the other men. And if you hadn't fought so well, what would they have done to you?"

She stared at him. "I understand. It makes sense. But here—"she touched over her heart "—tells me I took their lives. Connor didn't threaten my life."

His mouth hardened.

She sucked in a breath. "I was so focused on freeing us,

126

that I took those lives. Me. It wasn't to save my own life." Tears trickled down her cheeks. "I got caught up in my goal, and that's all that mattered. I never wanted to use my abilities to hurt anyone, but I guess I'm more like my birth father than I ever thought I was."

He cupped her cheek and kissed the top of her head. "You're not. It's the circumstances. Why don't you try to get more sleep?"

She couldn't imagine being all alone in this. Being summoned by Connor, doing his bidding, and no one to offer support. Alone in this room twenty-three hours a day. She would have curled up in a ball and starved herself.

"All right. I still feel exhausted." He helped her to her feet, and she rinsed her mouth, then trudged back to bed, with the hope that more nightmares wouldn't plague her.

***

It never would have crossed Theron's mind that Jamie could be missing for twenty-four days. When she was taken, he thought they'd have her back in hours, and surely not more than a couple of days. The only thing keeping him going was feeling her in his heart. Knowing she was still alive kept his hope up, and kept him moving through the days.

He helped Shauna set the kitchen table and carried the casserole while she brought in corn muffins. Besides minor things like this, he felt totally useless. Everything felt useless when they weren't going out to find Jamie.

"Thanks, Theron."

He shrugged. "I help where I can. Mostly, I feel like I'm in your way here."

She squeezed his forearm. "We're practically family, and we're in this together."

The front door closed and Theron waited for Jason to enter.

Jason kissed Shauna's cheek. "Honey, that smells delicious."

A small smile touched her lips. "It's a new recipe. Enchilada Casserole. Looking up recipes is a good distraction."

No mention of Jamie. Like a normal day. For everybody else. For him, it might never be normal again. Was this the point where, when someone disappears, everybody starts accepting it as the new normal? Even Jamie's parents had stopped calling every day. He couldn't do that to her.

They sat and dished up food. Jason talked about a case he was working on, not giving names, of course. He stuttered when he mentioned the client's sister, so his mind wasn't totally on that case.

Theron knew there wasn't much they could do for Jamie right now, but it rankled that Jason worked another case when his sister was more important. At least he called Mark daily to prod him for updates.

Theron set his fork on the empty plate and leaned back, lacing his fingers over his stomach. "Thank you, Shauna. That was great."

"Thanks, Theron."

Jason's phone trilled, and all eyes went to it, beside his plate. He swiped and punched. "Hi, Mark. You're on speaker. Me, Theron and Shauna."

"Hi, all. I've got weird news I figured you should hear."

Jason caught Theron's eye. "Yeah. We like weird. What do you have?"

"Six male bodies found. Man's dog started digging them up in the woods."

Jason frowned. "Six at once is a little weird, but that doesn't seem weird enough for a call."

"First off, the bodies were found less than five miles from where Walter Travers washed up."

Theron placed his forearms on the table and leaned forward.

"And the weird part is, two of the bodies had burns on the neck in the shape of hands."

Theron's eyes met Jason's, and he mouthed 'Jamie'. Jason nodded.

Theron eyed the phone. "What was cause of death of those two?"

"Coroner said the carotid artery was fried."

Theron closed his eyes and tipped his head up. He couldn't imagine what Jamie had gone through to do something like that. How had it affected her? He wished he could have protected her from it, or be with her to deal with the aftermath.

"What's the time of death?" Jason asked.

"Three to four days."

His trance thing. "That's—"

Jason glared and held his hand up. "I want to see the bodies."

"Four have been collected by next of kin. The other two aren't identified yet."

"Does one of those left have the burns?" Jason asked.

"Yeah."

Jason leaned closer to the phone. "Mark, get me in there."

"All right. I'll call you back with details."

Theron pushed to his feet, but leaned on the table. "Jason, that coincides with that-that whatever I felt from Jamie."

"I know, and I didn't want Mark to suspect that Jamie killed them. Let him think one of the bad guys did it."

A knife twisted in his gut. He never wanted it to get out that Jamie could have killed those men. An ordinary person would be more afraid of the act than understand that she did it in self-defense.

Jason clapped him on the shoulder. "We'll head out first thing in the morning."

"Yes!"

***

Jamie rinsed her mouth as Adam leaned against the closed bathroom door with his arms crossed. The queasiness was almost past.

"Jamie, that's three mornings in a row, *and* lunch yesterday. You can't blame this on your guilt over killing those guys."

"I know." She really had thought that was the reason the first day. Not any more. Theron's baby grew inside her. It was almost a surprise the baby had survived all the turmoil and stress she'd been through.

He glanced under the sink at the unopened box of sanitary pads. "Are you...pregnant?"

She was late, but who wouldn't be with the stress of being imprisoned and wondering if you'd die? Three mornings of vomiting and mostly feeling fine otherwise, gave her a big clue. And she had felt tired, which she had attributed to being depressed.

"Maybe. Please, don't tell anybody."

He squatted beside her and covered her hand. "I wouldn't, but one of the guards heard you throwing up yesterday and asked me about it. I told him that I felt a little queasy, too, and maybe the ham was bad."

She gave him a weak smile. "Thanks for covering."

"Come on. Let's see if you can eat something."

Jamie managed to eat two pieces of toast as Adam ate with his normal gusto.

Theron should have been the first one to hear the news. If

she didn't get out of there, he might never find out. She rubbed a hand over her flat stomach. What would Connor do if he found out? If she knew what his plans were for her, she'd have an idea how this baby would affect them. She'd do whatever was necessary to protect this little life.

Keys rattled in the lock and the door swung open. There was still a half-hour before her gym time.

A guard stepped in with an older man behind him. "Adam. Gym. Now."

Adam jumped up and stood between Jamie and the other men. "I'm not leaving Jamie with a stranger."

The short and a bit overweight man stepped to the side of the guard. He swung out a black bag. "I'm a doctor."

Jamie's heart pounded. Her secret wouldn't be a secret much longer.

Adam faced her. "Jamie—"

She stood. "You better go." There wasn't anything he could do.

The doctor didn't give his name. He had her sit on a kitchen chair and took her blood pressure. He checked her heart and breathing, and flashed a light in her eyes. He pulled a cup from his bag. "Pee in this and leave it on the bathroom counter."

She took it with resignation, knowing what he'd do with it. Too bad Adam wasn't around for a substitute.

She returned from the bathroom and the doctor disappeared inside. A few minutes later, he came out, and stopped beside the end of the bed. "Sit here, please."

She complied. What else could she do?

"Now, lie back."

She stared at the ceiling as he palpated her stomach, then pulled her shirt back down. "You can sit up now."

He went to the door. "You can come in."

She thought she'd see Adam, but Connor entered. She bit

131

her lip, and counted her breaths to keep them under control. Maybe that would help slow her pounding heart.

Connor squinted his eyes at her. "What's wrong with her?"

"She's pregnant."

Connor grinned. "Is she?"

"Six or seven weeks."

Connor whipped his head to the doctor. "Seven weeks? Get rid of it."

Jamie covered her stomach with her hand. Not that it would protect the baby.

"I've never done an abortion. If I tried, I could kill her or make her sterile."

They talked as if this baby was worse than nothing. This little life was a link to Theron. She couldn't let them take it.

"Then find someone who can."

The doctor tucked his head down and gave a quick nod. "I'll call you when I've arranged it."

A short reprieve.

Connor pointed at her. "You will carry no man's child, but Adam's." He stalked out of the room.

Jamie stared at the closed door, her heart pounding. Her baby. She'd just been confirmed pregnant, and in the next moment Connor ordered her baby's death. She rubbed her hand over her stomach. She needed to protect her child.

Connor had confirmed it. One reason for her kidnapping was so she would have Adam's baby. Given enough time together, Connor must have figured she and Adam would have sex and she'd get pregnant.

Was there something special about the two of them? About a baby the two of them would make? She shook her head.

Did Adam know that's what his purpose here was? Had he been a willing participant from the first? Or was he in the dark like she'd been? At least he hadn't forced himself on her. She shivered.

If her baby somehow survived the second doctor, she couldn't bring down the building with lightning. She had to protect her baby's life.

The door opened and Adam rushed to kneel in front of her, taking her hands. "Jamie, are you all right?"

"For now. The doctor confirmed I'm pregnant." She squinted at him. "Connor was excited about it until he found out it's not yours, and then he told the doctor to find someone to get rid of it." She pulled her hands from his. "Adam, why does Connor want me to have your baby? Is this the whole reason we're here?"

Adam ran a hand through his hair. "I can't help what Connor wants." He took her hand again. "Jamie, I'm your friend. I know that's what you want, so that's what you get. I would never force myself on you."

"Thank you."

Chapter 15

Theron rolled his eyes as Jason pulled into the dirt parking lot for Grimm Conservation Trust. "Seriously? They buried the bodies here?"

Jason shrugged. "Somebody's got a warped sense of humor."

They'd left Jason's house at seven. It was now nearly ten o'clock. They'd spent the last fifteen minutes on a windy road with cracked, pot-holed pavement.

They got out of the SUV as Jason stared at the map on his phone, then pointed at an opening in the woods. "It's that way about a quarter mile." He bypassed a sign with a map and description of the area, and took off down the dirt trail. Trees came to the edge of the six foot wide path and the branches provided a canopy overhead. If the parking lot had been empty when the vehicles arrived, no one would have seen the men moving the grisly evidence.

Theron followed behind, hoping they'd find something the police had missed.

Jason checked his phone every few steps. He veered off the path onto a narrower one and stopped after about fifty feet. A short distance off the path, the dirt had been disturbed.

Theron inspected the ground. "Looks like they didn't miss anything." He stepped closer and squatted down. Dirt was pushed into mounds around a hole in the ground. He wrinkled his nose as the odor of decay assailed him.

Jason pulled a small gardening shovel from his back pocket and shifted the loose dirt into new piles. Nothing more than a few small stones surfaced. Some of the dirt stuck together in dark clumps, and Theron shivered at the thought that it might be blood.

A few days ago, the men who had been buried here had seen Jamie. She had likely taken the lives of two of them. If only he could touch those dark clumps and get a sense of Jamie's whereabouts. He hated that this pile of dirt was the closest he'd been to her in weeks.

He stood. "I'm going to look a little farther up the trail."

Jason waved him off.

The path had become single file and every so often, a footprint marked the edge of the trail. Theron wondered if they could have been left by one of the men who deposited the bodies. A pair of imprints stopped him. He peered into the woods, finding dead leaves disturbed to about four feet in. The guy probably had to relieve himself.

Theron studied the ground as he followed the shuffled path, kicking leaves away in case anything had been dropped. Not likely.

At the end of the disturbance, two side-by-side footprints had sunk into the soft earth. He shifted the leaves and searched.

"Yes!" He reached for the brown lucky rabbit's foot and paused above it. No, there wouldn't be fingerprints on the fur. He scooped it up and felt the slight tingle of a protection spell. The owner must be associated with the kidnappers. "Dude, your luck just ran out."

He hurried back to the burial site.

Jason stood over the hole, dusting his hands together.

Theron kept his prize hidden. "Find anything?"

Jason stared into the grave. "No. I didn't expect to, but I wanted to cover all our bases."

"I did."

Jason frowned. "Did what?"

Theron held out the rabbit's foot on his palm. "Found this."

Jason squinted at it. "Any hiker could have dropped that."

Theron grinned. "Uh-uh. There's a protection spell on it."

Jason's eyes widened. "Maybe Mom can pull something from it."

"That would be great!" Theron slipped it into his pocket.

Jason turned toward the trail. "Let's keep an eye out for anything else on our way back to the car."

They retraced their steps at a slower pace, and Theron checked the edges of the trail for anything that may have been dropped. He didn't think they'd have much luck since the police would have combed over the trail leading to the burial. He spotted a shiny object, but on closer inspection found a faded, old Coke can a few feet off the trail.

Almost back to the parking area, Jason's phone rang, and he stopped. "Hi, Mom."

Theron couldn't hear Kathleen's voice.

"But, I thought…Hold on. I'm putting you on speaker." He swiped the phone and held it between the two of them. "Okay. I thought you couldn't read a history on people."

"I can't. But, um, they're dead. So they aren't really people anymore."

Jason shook his head. "Now you think you're a necromancer?"

For a few seconds, it raised Theron's hopes, but Jason's disbelieving voice sent it plummeting again.

Her sigh came through the phone. "Don't you think it's worth a try?"

"At this point, anything's worth a try. Oh, and Theron

136

found a rabbit's foot with a protection spell. Do you think you can read it?"

"I should be able to. Your dad and I can be there in…two-and-a-half hours."

"All right. We'll see you at the motel." Jason tucked his phone away.

Theron shoved his hands in his front pockets. "What do you think the chances are that she can do it?"

Jason shrugged. "She's really good at reading the history of objects. She's gone back centuries. But, dead bodies? Your guess is as good as mine."

Jamie had said her mom had strong abilities. He hoped that proved true. Nothing else had worked out so far. In a sense, he felt closer to Jamie, but he didn't know how that could be. They still had no idea where to look for her.

***

Theron paced Jason's motel room, from the bathroom to the bed. Six steps.

Kathleen and Reese had arrived fifteen minutes ago. Jason sat on the foot of the bed, his mother on the desk chair, and Reese leaned against the desk.

Turn. Six steps. Turn. Six steps.

Kathleen held the rabbit's foot, her eyes closed. "I'm sorry it's taking so long. Apparently, the spell is blocking the history, but the shield is getting thinner." Her face pinched.

Theron could feel the extra energy she expended. Turn. Six steps. Turn.

Kathleen's face had cleared to a neutral expression. "He's playing with this as he sits beside the driver in a car with dark leather. The car stops and he slips it into his pocket." She sighed. "Let me see if I can go farther back."

Six steps to the bed. Turn. Three steps.

"He's in a kind of office lounge."

Turn.

"Tables with metal chairs and padded seats. A couch against the wall. The TV is on. No windows. It feels like an interior room. I'll try farther back."

Three steps. Theron dropped onto the bed beside Jason, leaned forward, elbows on his thighs.

"A gray haired woman is reciting a protection spell. She hands the rabbit's foot to the new owner." Kathleen opened her eyes and shook her head. "Sorry I couldn't get more."

Jason stood and kissed his mother's forehead. "You did great. You can't get what's not there." He swiped the rabbit's foot from her hand and dropped it in the trash.

***

Theron stood beside Kathleen and Reese near the door as Jason handed over some papers and talked to the attendant at the morgue. Mark had set up an appointment with the excuse that Kathleen worked at another morgue that held a body with similar burns.

Jason turned to them. "This way."

They followed the attendant into a cold room with drawers. Way too many drawers. Theron wondered how many hid bodies. How many had died at the hands of another like the ones they were checking?

The man referenced a clipboard hanging on the wall and pulled open a drawer. His eyes traveled over their group, probably wondering why it took four people to exam a body. The man left, closing the door behind him.

Jason pulled back the sheet, revealing a man in his late twenties with a four-day-old beard. A burn in the shape of a small hand covered his throat. "Okay, Mom. Do your thing."

Having heard how two of the men died, hadn't prepared

Theron for seeing the handprint on this man's throat. His own throat tightened. The handprint matched the many branches Jamie had burned. She really had killed this man. For all the practice he put her through, he never expected she'd end up using her ability to kill, had hoped she'd only need it to injure. His heart ached at the thought that she'd had to protect her life. The fear she must have felt to have no other choice. He wished he'd been there to help her through the aftermath.

What happened after she'd killed the men? The others now knew what she could do. How would they have subdued her to keep her captive?

Kathleen paled when her eyes dropped to the dead man's face, and she turned her head into Reese's shoulder.

He put an arm around her. "Honey, you don't have to do this."

"I have to. For Jamie." Her hand hovered over the body's arm for several seconds. She took a deep breath and grasped it, closing her eyes.

Theron was relieved that Kathleen's vision would start after the man's death, if it worked. He wouldn't want her to experience the pain of watching her daughter kill a man. He gave Kathleen points for her bravery to go through this to rescue her daughter.

Quiet had seeped into the cold room of death. It startled Theron when Kathleen spoke in a low, almost trance-like voice. "He's on the floor of a huge room. Maybe it's a conference room. Jamie! Jamie's sitting with her back to a door, crying." As she spoke the last word, tears streaked her own cheeks.

Theron's throat choked up. His Jamie needed him.

"Two men are cutting the throats of unconscious men on the floor. One says that one of them is already dead, and the other man says the same of this one and gives Jamie a thumbs up. She drops her head to her knees."

Six men in the room, two killed by Jamie's hands. What did the evil guy try to do? Did Jamie cry because she killed the men or because of something they'd done to her?

The silence ate at him, and Theron wondered if that was all they'd get. They were so much closer, but not close enough to rescue Jamie.

Jason and Reese's eyes were on Kathleen, hope shining through.

Kathleen's breaths came in quick pants. Struggling to hold onto her vision or to not give in and let go, he didn't know which. "Men are carrying out the bodies to cars. One is an SUV and the other is a sedan. This man and another are placed in the trunk of the sedan. The others are put in the SUV. Now it's dark."

Kathleen pulled her hand away and Reese wrapped his arms around her. She dropped her head to his shoulder. After a minute, she lifted it and took a deep breath, turning to them. "I saw the building. It's a brick single-story, office type building. It doesn't look old."

Jason touched his mother's shoulder. "Did you happen to get the license plate numbers?"

She shook her head. "I didn't think to look. Sorry."

She'd gotten a lot of details. Theron couldn't blame her for missing the plate numbers. He probably wouldn't have done as well.

She bit her lip. "I could try again."

Jason gripped her arm. "Are you up to it?"

She pushed her shoulders back. "It'll only be the last couple of minutes."

Kathleen gripped the dead arm without hesitation, and closed her eyes.

Theron's hands tingled, and he realized that he'd gripped them into tight fists. He flexed his fingers, and waited for one small detail that could take them to Jamie. He leaned forward when Kathleen spoke.

"I see the plates." She rattled off the numbers and pulled her arm back. Her knees gave out and Reese tightened his hold on her.

Jason hugged his mother and kissed her cheek. "Thanks, Mom. That was great. I'll see if Mark can track down the owners. And we'll check Google Earth for the building, circling out from the burial site, but it's a lot of area to cover."

She grabbed Jason's arm. "Wait. I just thought of something. I can read one of the men they put in the SUV. Maybe I'll catch street signs." She nodded her head toward the body. "This guy got put into a car trunk, so it went dark, but I might see more from one of the guys in the SUV."

Jason hurried to the door and grabbed the clipboard beside it. "Do you remember what they looked like?" He scanned the page. "This one came in the same day he did. Drawer twenty-four."

Theron didn't think Kathleen had enough energy to make another reading, but she'd probably do it until she collapsed if it would rescue her daughter.

Reese pulled the drawer open and flung back a sheet.

Kathleen shook her head. "He was in the trunk, too."

Jason covered the body closest to him and pushed the drawer closed. Reese did the same with the other.

"Okay. If the plate numbers don't work out, I'll have Mark find out the addresses for the funeral homes. Now let's get out of here."

Theron hugged Kathleen. "Thank you."

She cupped his cheek. "We *are* getting our girl back."

They'd gotten more from this expedition than Theron expected. Now the new information had to lead somewhere.

***

Jamie woke with sore arms and tried to shift. It was still dark, but it didn't take light to know her wrists were tied to the headboard. She pulled harder, only to feel ropes cut into her skin.

"Adam? Are you awake?"

"Mmm. What the? I'm tied up. How did this happen?"

Jamie turned her head. If the light was on, the room would have spun. "They must have put drugs in our food last night."

Adam growled. "Yeah, my heads a little fuzzy. I don't remember much after dinner."

She kicked the covers off. "I'm wearing yesterday's clothes." She couldn't hold back her tears. "I think they're going to take the baby today." She'd only known for a few days, but she already loved her child, Theron's child.

They planned to invade her body and steal the little life from her. There was a chance, like the other doctor had been afraid of, that this more experienced doctor could slip up and she'd never have children again. Connor didn't care what happened as long as he got what he wanted.

"Jamie, I'm so sorry."

The lights turned on, seven o'clock, and she wiped her cheeks on her sleeves. She couldn't let them kill her baby. She had to break the vow she'd made when she was eleven.

She studied Adam. He'd become a good friend over these weeks. He'd kept her sane. "Why do you think they tied you up?"

"They know I'd untie you."

Keys rattled at the door and Jamie tensed, fear sliced through her. It was too soon. She wasn't ready for this.

Crooked-nose stood at the door as Blondie approached, and opened a knife. She wanted to close her eyes, but she watched every step. He went to Adam's side of the bed. Maybe they didn't think Adam was serving his purpose, and the guard would plunge the knife into Adam's chest. Her eyes went to Adam's face. He didn't look afraid. She wasn't that brave.

The knife flashed toward Adam's head.

"No!" She struggled against the ropes. They couldn't kill Adam. It was bad enough watching the bad guys get their throats cut, but not her friend.

The knife passed over Adam's head and cut the ropes binding him to the bed. "You're going to the gym for a while."

Adam threw himself over Jamie. "No. I'm staying with Jamie."

"That's not the plan." Blondie flashed the knife, grabbed Adam's arm and yanked him from the bed. "Go."

Adam looked back at her, his eyes tight, as the guard dragged him from her sight. Crooked-nose pulled the door closed.

She waited fifteen interminable minutes before the door opened again.

A man with a medical bag waltzed in, followed by a woman. He stopped halfway to the bed. "I didn't expect her to be tied." He continued to the bed and set down his bag.

"You don't have to do this. Please don't." Jamie didn't think begging would work, but she needed to give it a try first.

The doctor patted her foot. "Your father told me about the rape. I understand your hesitation, but this is for the best."

She sputtered. That's what the man wanted to believe? "He's not my father. I wasn't raped. Please don't take my baby." Tears coursed down her cheeks. What if she couldn't save the baby? Theron would lose his child before knowing there was one.

The doctor frowned, and rhythmically bumped his case against his leg. "Your father said you might lie. I'm sure afterwards you'll realize this was for the best."

There was no other choice now. She would have to compel him. Both of them. She pushed her fear away, knowing it might interfere with her power. A little bit of anger might help, though.

That's what had prompted her first accidental and only use of the ability when she was eleven. Andrew Johnson had teased her for weeks at school. She didn't even remember what about, except for that last time in front of the school. He said her mother was a cold-blooded killer. Anger exploded and she yelled at him. "Why don't you go play in traffic?" And to her horror, he did. Tires screeched on dry pavement as he darted into the busy street. She'd never forget the sound of his body being struck by a car and seeing his head hit the windshield. He suffered a broken leg and arm and a concussion and didn't remember why he was in the street.

Whenever she'd been tempted to use the ability, the memory of Andrew Johnson squashed the desire. Not this time. Today, she'd be saving a life. If the ability worked.

She built up anger at Connor for bringing her here, for taking her from Theron, for sending a doctor to kill her baby. Then she channeled it to the first push of thoughts into their minds. *You will not perform an abortion. You will see yourself go through the motions, think you are doing it, but will not harm the baby.*

"Natalie, let's get the sheet under her."

The assistant shook the protective sheet out and they slid it under Jamie's legs and lifted her slightly to slide it higher. She didn't know yet if they were responding. A dozen years had past since she last used this ability. Maybe it had faded away.

Natalie pulled a short pole out of the bag and telescoped it up, snapping the legs into place. She set it on the floor and picked up an IV bag, hanging it on the pole. She picked up the needle at the end of the line.

Just tape it to my arm. Don't push it into the skin. Tape it only. She waited for the needle prick.

The woman pulled a roll of tape from her pocket and taped the needle to Jamie's arm. She let out a slow, stress relieving breath. She'd reached the woman.

"Administer the sedative," the doctor said.

The assistant pulled a hypodermic needle out of a pocket of the bag, uncapped it, and shoved the needle into the drip under the bag, then pushed in the plunger.

Don't open the clamp.

Natalie touched the clamp on the line, but didn't open it. No liquid flooded the needle.

She feigned sleep, with her eyes open a crack. It would be harder for them to believe if she struggled and pleaded.

The doctor knelt at the foot of the bed and pulled instruments out of his bag. Not everybody could be compelled. Terror hit at the thought that she couldn't prevent him from aborting her baby, and now would feel every pain he inflicted to take it away from her.

It *had* to work.

She added desperation to her push. *Don't really do it. Imagine you're doing the abortion, but don't touch me.*

With his hands on his tools, he closed his eyes. Maybe it was working. Or maybe it bothered him to take a tiny life the mother had asked him not to and he had to prepare himself for it.

He picked up a speculum and Jamie tensed. She'd had a pelvic exam once and the doctor had used one. *Please. Imagine you're using it, but set it down.*

She jumped when the device ratcheted, and relaxed somewhat when he placed it on the bed.

Jamie studied Natalie. *Imagine you're helping the doctor the way you normally would.*

Jamie watched suspiciously, her heart pounding, expecting any second that something would go wrong. Someone could walk in, see the doctor wasn't doing his job, and stop her from compelling him. She didn't know how this ability worked. Could someone counter her commands? Maybe they'd knock her out. That would end it.

Breathe. Breathe. Slow, deep breaths. If she panicked, she might lose control of her ability. If it was even working on the doctor.

He pulled a small pan from his bag and set it on the bed. She watched through wary eyes. So far, he hadn't touched her. The doctor picked up a looped instrument and she took several shallow breaths. *Stop. Imagine it only.* He froze and closed his eyes then, dropped his instruments into the pan and stood. "I'll take care of this. Clean her up."

Metal instruments rattled as they fell into the sink, and the water turned on, then the toilet flushed.

Jamie dropped her head to the pillow, and let out a long breath, letting most of her tension leave with it. She wasn't out of the woods yet.

Natalie removed the tape and IV needle from Jamie's arm. She pulled a wet cloth from a package and touched it against Jamie's thigh, making her jump.

"Almost done." She pulled the protective sheet, partially folded it up, and pulled it the rest of the way from under Jamie. She completed folding it and stuffed it into a plastic bag. She checked Jamie's pulse, put a pressure cuff on her and checked it with a stethoscope. Her blood pressure must have been astronomical. "Just a bit high." She set it on the bed.

The assistant joined the doctor in the bathroom and they talked quietly for a few minutes. They returned to the room and packed the bag.

Natalie touched Jamie's forehead, checked her down

below, and took her blood pressure again. "Everything's good. Let's get you covered up so you can rest."

At the exit, the doctor frowned back at her before knocking. The door opened and they were gone.

Jamie relaxed her tense muscles. It worked! She never wanted to go through something like that again. Her energy had been wiped out, exhaustion pulling at her. She feigned sleep as Blondie came in. She peeked through her eyelashes, and saw he had a knife like before. She wasn't afraid of it this time as he cut through the ropes.

It took everything in her not to flinch when the man brought her arms down, and rubbed her cheek. "I'm so sorry, Jamie."

She was surprised at his reaction. His footsteps faded away and the door closed.

She rubbed her sore shoulders. A surge of elation ran through her. The first time she'd intentionally compelled anyone and it had worked on two people. She rubbed a hand across her stomach. Her little one was still alive because of this scary ability.

At fourteen, it had taken weeks of surreptitious searches through her mother's witchcraft books to find out anything about compelling people. It seemed to be a rare ability, even rarer in women. Not surprising, since so many men with the ability used it like a date rape drug.

People with strong abilities couldn't be compelled, so that probably meant it wouldn't work on Connor. Not all ordinary people were susceptible and there was no way to know before trying it.

Maybe she could test it in little ways to find out who it worked on. One on one, she could get away with it, even if it didn't work, but there were always at least two guards. What if one guard was affected and not the other? And a group? She'd been exhausted compelling two people.

She yawned. Fatigue dragged her into a dark place, and she fell asleep before Adam returned.

Chapter 16

The four of them had gone to breakfast at a diner near the motel. They sat in a worn booth next to the window. Theron forced down half his food. They were so close to finding Jamie, he didn't feel like eating and didn't want to take the time, but he needed to keep up his strength.

Jason wouldn't tell them what information Mark had sent until they'd eaten and he could do it privately. Theron glanced at the other three nearly empty plates, and then at Jason. "Okay. Spill."

Jason scanned the room. There had been one other table with occupants when they arrived, but now the room was half full. "Let's go out to my car."

Reese dropped money on the table and they left.

They settled inside the car, Kathleen in front with Jason, Theron behind Jason and Reese behind his wife.

Jason turned, and looked at each of them. "I talked to Mark this morning. First off, the sedan was owned by Walter Travers. That's a dead end. The SUV is owned by The CR Salem Group with offices in downtown Boston. That's not where Jamie's being held. The company is owned by a holding company at the same address, but different suite. Mark's still working on it."

Theron's heart sunk. He'd pinned his hopes on the car

registrations giving them Jamie's location, and they'd rescue her today.

Jason studied his mother.

Dark shadows under Kathleen's eyes revealed she hadn't slept well, or was still not fully recovered from reading the body the day before.

Jason's lips thinned. "Mark sent pictures of the other bodies and the locations of the funeral homes. Mom, are you okay doing this again? It looked pretty hard on you yesterday. We can wait to see if Mark finds the owner of The CR Salem Group."

"No!" They couldn't wait. They'd waited long enough. Reading the body was more of a sure thing now than waiting to find the owner. And what if the owner had no connection to Jamie?

Kathleen glanced at Theron, Reese and her son again. "I don't want to wait, and those bodies are there now."

Jason pulled out his phone, and handed it to her.

Kathleen scrolled through the pictures, turned the phone and handed it back to Jason. "Any but this one. They put him in first, so his body probably didn't have a good view."

Jason scrolled through the others. "All right. We'll see Jeffery Schofield. They don't have morning viewing hours, but we'll convince them that his aunt has an emergency and can't stay until the afternoon. That should give us some privacy." He checked his watch. "Let's get there just after nine."

Jason drove past the funeral home. A block from it, he made a u-turn and parked at the curb. They still had fifteen minutes before it opened. "We'll stay here until it's time. I don't want anyone peeking out and wondering why we're not coming in." He turned to face Kathleen. "You'll have to pretend you're this guy's aunt. Think you're up to it?"

"I'd do anything to rescue Jamie. It shouldn't be as bad

this time. I won't have to go back to that conference room again." A shiver passed through her. "I'll start outside."

Theron's heart swelled with love for this woman. He was glad that Jamie had grown up with so much love from all her family.

An uncomfortable silence filled the vehicle, and every few minutes, Jason checked his watch.

Tension tightened Theron's neck and shoulders. The funeral home staff might not let them in until viewing hours. They might only let Kathleen in, which would make it difficult, since she'd appeared to be in a trance the day before. They might need to take notes of the location, if she found it. Maybe something would be different this time and it wouldn't work at all.

Finally, Jason tapped the steering wheel. "It's time."

He started the car and drove into the parking lot next to the funeral home. They entered the building as a group, but stayed near the door as Jason went in search of someone to talk to. Five minutes later, he returned with a woman.

"Ms. Schofield. I'm so sorry about your nephew. Let me show you to his room." She placed an arm around Kathleen's shoulders, led her down a short hall, and into a room with couches and chairs set around the walls. She opened the coffin.

Kathleen's shoulders shook. "Jeff." Reese put an arm around his wife.

If Theron didn't know the truth, he would have thought Kathleen was grieving.

The woman's sympathetic expression touched each of them. "I'll give you some time alone."

Jason gave her a quick nod. "Thank you."

Kathleen stepped forward and covered the folded hands with one of her own, closing her eyes.

A flesh colored cloth covered the man's neck. Theron

didn't know if this was one whose neck had been cut or if Jamie had touched him. He looked more like he was asleep than the bodies at the morgue.

Kathleen spoke in a low voice. "They placed him in the back of the SUV and I can see through the windows."

Theron bowed his head, but kept his eyes on Kathleen. He figured it couldn't hurt to appear as if he was praying.

"We drove about a half block and turned right. I see the roofs of lots of houses. I think it's a subdivision. We stopped beside a stop sign. Bridge Street. I see Bridge Street! We're taking a right onto it."

Reese rubbed her arm and shushed her.

Jason had his phone out, tapping in notes.

Kathleen inhaled. "We're going too fast. Let me see if I can slow it down." Her forehead wrinkled. "Okay. We're passing Fairfield Street. Oh, I missed that one. There's Commonwealth Ave and Hillcrest Ave. Now that I'm used to this, I'm going back to the beginning to see if I can catch any of the first roads."

Theron waited expectantly. She'd named a lot of roads. It must narrow down the area. He was pretty sure he would be able to feel Jamie more if they were close.

"Okay. There's that quick right turn, and the subdivision. Oh, I can't catch the other side of the sign. There. The next street is Arbor Lane." Kathleen opened her eyes. "Jason, do you think that's enough?"

Jason kissed his mother's cheek. "That was great, Mom. Let's get out of here and I'll check the maps."

A large man filled the doorway, anger in his eyes. "Who the hell are you?"

Theron stiffened and his heart made a double beat before settling into middle-of-competition mode.

Jason hurried across the room. "Mr. Schofield?" Jason held out his hand. "I'm Jason. I was a friend of Jeff's." He pointed over his shoulder. "He used to call my mom Aunt Kat."

The man shook Jason's hand, appearing slightly mollified.

Theron was relieved he didn't have to come up with a lie for being here.

Jason held his keys out to Reese. "Why don't the three of you go out to the car and let me chat with Mr. Schofield? I'll be right out."

Theron had to work at keeping a slow pace. He didn't want to make Mr. Schofield suspicious because he ran out the door.

They settled into the car.

Reese's leg jiggled up and down. "Let's give him five minutes and then call the police." He checked his watch.

Not a comforting thought. He didn't think they'd done anything they could be arrested for, but there was no way to explain why they were there.

"Five minutes." Reese pulled his phone out.

"Reese, wait!" Kathleen called out.

The door had opened and Jason stood in the doorway. He talked to someone they couldn't see. His hand went out, like he was shaking another person's hand. He turned and walked towards them, making a thumbs up in front of his body.

He got in the car and started driving.

Kathleen grabbed his upper arm. "Jason. What happened?"

"I told Mr. Schofield I hadn't seen Jeff in a couple of months. He said that Jeff had disappeared a week before his body was found. He'd missed a date with his girlfriend and dinner with his parents."

A chill filled Theron's chest. "If he was kidnapped, he didn't volunteer for whatever happened with Jamie, and maybe the others didn't either. Maybe Jamie killed two guys

153

who were just as trapped as she was."

"I'm not telling her that," Jason said.

"I'm never telling her." She was probably having a hard enough time dealing with killing guys who were trying to harm her. What would it do to her to find out they were forced into it by the bad guys?

***

Jamie forced her eyes open. Adam lay at her back and she scooted a bit away from him. The lights were on, and the clock read eight-forty-three. Day or night? She couldn't believe how bad she had to pee. She slid out of bed and headed to the bathroom.

Adam was sitting up when she came back out. "They must have really knocked you out yesterday."

She dropped onto the foot of the bed. "Yesterday? I slept all day yesterday and through the night?" Between compelling the doctor and assistant, her anxiety over protecting the baby, and the pregnancy itself, she must have expended every ounce of energy she possessed.

He leaned forward and covered her hand. "How do you feel?"

She cast her eyes down, not wanting him to see the truth in them. "I'm okay." She slipped her hand from his and crossed her arms on her chest.

Keys rattled in the door and it swung open. A guard carried in a tray and set it on the table. "Good. You're awake. No gym today, Jamie." He picked up the previous tray and left.

Adam spoke in a gentle voice. "Are you ready to eat? It's been like thirty-six hours since your last meal."

Her stomach growled and she headed to the table. She sat and lifted the cover on one plate. The smell of eggs turned her stomach and she rushed to the bathroom.

Adam followed her and closed the door as she vomited. He wet a washcloth and squatted down beside her, handing her the cloth. He spoke, barely above a whisper. "You're still pregnant, aren't you?"

She bit her lip and nodded. "Don't tell them."

"I won't. I would have stopped them before if I could. How did you do it?"

She stared at the washcloth in her hands. "I don't want to talk about it." If Connor found out she had the ability to compel…she didn't want to think about what he'd try to force her to do.

He squinted, and stared for several seconds. "All right." He stood and held out his hand. "You really need to eat something."

"It's the eggs. If I don't have to smell them, I might be able to eat."

He closed the lid on the toilet, flushed and held his hand out again.

She took it, and stood.

Adam pointed to the lid. "Sit. Give me five minutes to eat all the eggs, then you can come out."

"Thanks. I'll take a shower." Now, if she could tone down her stomach problems to just nausea, she could probably hide her pregnancy for a while longer, but there would be a time when it was obvious she was still pregnant. And then what? She had to get out before that.

Adam seemed so understanding. It didn't sound like he minded that she was pregnant with another man's child. She still didn't know why Connor wanted her to have Adam's baby, and only realized later that Adam hadn't answered that question. Maybe he didn't know or maybe he didn't want to tell her. She was frustrated, but didn't know if she should confront him with it again.

***

Theron stared anxiously at the passing streets. After twenty-six days, they were finally close. He could feel Jamie more intensely. One more day, and he'd have her in his arms again.

Kathleen pointed. "There's Hillcrest!"

Reese leaned forward and squeezed his wife's shoulder. The tightness had left his mouth.

Jason slowed. He had put the intersection of Arbor Lane and Bridge Street into his GPS, and the cross streets in Dedham came up. Forty-five minutes later, the street names Kathleen had called out appeared on signs.

Theron watched the GPS as they approached Arbor Lane. The following street name came into view. Breede Terrace. They were almost there. They had to be.

They passed Arbor and Jason took a left onto Breede.

"These are the roofs I saw." Kathleen swiveled her head from one side to the other. She pointed ahead. "Turn left up there."

The street ended at another street and Jason took the turn. He slowed further.

Theron watched both sides of the road for the brick building Kathleen had mentioned.

Her voice filled the cabin. "That's it! That's it!"

Jason continued to drive by as they all stared at the long building.

"I want to reach out to her," Kathleen said.

"Not now, Mom. She might get too excited and give it away. Tomorrow. You can contact her shortly before we go in."

She fell back in the seat. "Okay."

Jason had told Theron how, when he and his parents were rescuing Shauna, his mother was able to speak into Shauna's mind. They had Shauna convince her ex to pull over for a bathroom break. Kathleen's range seemed to have been about a half mile.

Theron leaned toward the building. He wished they could go in right now. They were so close. He'd reluctantly agreed that it was better to wait for backup. No telling what kind of abilities the people inside might have. The police could be worse than worthless.

"I can feel her. She's in there." He hoped nothing happened overnight. He'd be devastated if, in the morning, he couldn't feel her in the building because she'd been moved, or worse, if he lost the sense of her before they came back.

His head understood that the four of them couldn't go in blind right now, not knowing how many men were inside and if they had destructive abilities, but his heart was ready to reclaim Jamie.

Kathleen turned around, held her hand out to him, and he took it. "It's been such a comfort knowing you could feel her. Knowing she's alive."

"I don't think I could have survived without feeling her." It was hard enough wondering if they'd hurt her.

She squeezed his hand. "I'm glad she has someone who loves her so much."

They reached a circle at the end of the road and Jason turned around, then stopped. "All right. I tagged the location. I'm sending it to Mark so he can, hopefully, get blue prints for us. He's confirmed that his team will be here tomorrow morning."

"Yes!" Theron's elation ran through him. Jamie had been in that evil man's hands way too long.

Chapter 17

Theron counted the vehicles parked in the parking lot of the building that held Jamie. Eight cars. If each car represented one person, they'd overtake the building in no time. Jason followed Mark's SUV and his two men, past the building.

Theron wished they could go in immediately, but Jason had decided that, since the building looked like an office, they'd wait until nine o'clock to hit it. Likely, the doors would be unlocked by then. If not, Mark said they'd shoot the glass out of the doors. Not a great option since that would draw everybody out at once.

Once they entered the wooded area, out of sight of the building, Jason stopped the SUV. "Mom, can you reach Jamie from here?"

"I think so." Kathleen closed her eyes.

Theron knew Jamie was in there and that she was alive, but didn't know her condition. Her kidnapper could have tortured her every day of her captivity. His gut twisted at the thought that she could have been in pain for weeks. He sucked in a breath. They'd have her out of there soon.

After a few minutes, a smile lit Kathleen's face. "She's okay. I told her to hold on for just a bit longer. She said she's in the basement with another hostage named Adam. Take a left from the front doors."

Jason continued to the end of the road. He reached into his glove compartment, pulled out a handful of zip ties and held them over the backseat. "Here, Theron. You'll need these."

"Thanks." Theron stuck them in his pants pocket. He'd take great pleasure in knocking around a few people before putting zip ties on them.

They all got out of the cars. Mark unrolled the building plans and spread them on the hood of his car. He'd sent them to Jason's phone that morning when they discussed the plan, but they hadn't been detailed enough.

"Jamie's in the basement," Jason said.

Mark raised his eyebrows. "And you know this how?"

They stared at each other for several seconds. Mark shook his head. "Never mind."

Jason had said they'd worked together, and Mark knew some of his secrets.

Mark turned back to the plans and pointed at the entrance. "Zack and Trey are going in first. They'll clear the foyer and head to the right. Jason and Theron, head to the left." He dropped his index finger onto the plans. "The stairs to the basement are here." He glanced at them. "Look for other hostages, too, and bring them all out."

They hadn't told Mark about Adam. Would there be more prisoners? Once they found Jamie, Theron's only plan was to bring her out safely. He'd let Jason handle the rest.

Reese cleared his throat. "I'd like to go in first."

Jason grabbed Reese's arm. "Dad, no!"

"No, sir," Mark said. "You and the missus aren't going in at all."

Reese held up his hand. "Hear me out. I can make a potion to become invisible." Mark's men snickered. "I'll put the people I find into a catatonic state, then you guys can tie them up. They won't know what hit them."

Theron had never heard of such a potion, but Reese wasn't crazy. He was a father who would do anything for his daughter. Mark and his men probably thought Reese was loony. But it was a great way to sneak into a building.

Kathleen stepped between the men and stood in front of Reese, gripping his arms tightly. "Reese, you can't. What happens if you go blind before it's over?"

Jason pushed Reese's shoulder, so he faced him. "What does Mom mean about you going blind?"

"It's all right, son. I've done this before. The potion that renders me invisible has a side effect after the hour is up of making me blind for the next hour. It's not a big deal, and an hour should be long enough to take control of the building."

Kathleen sighed, and kissed Reese's cheek. "Be careful. I don't want to lose you."

Reese hugged her. "You won't." He glanced at Jason. "Open the back."

"I wouldn't want to risk going blind." Trey patted his gun. "I'll just rely on my buddy here."

With a click of Jason's remote, the SUV hatch opened and Reese unzipped a bag, pulling out a vial of powder and a flask with an inch of liquid in it. Next, he removed a Bunsen burner and set it on the ground, starting a flame. He poured the powder from the vial into the liquid, swirled it, then set it on the burner.

While that heated, he reached into the bag and pulled out another vial, this one with a viscous yellow liquid. "This is the catatonic potion." He waved it. "This and a few words will make a person as stiff as a statue."

Reese glanced at his burner, then checked his watch. "Just a minute now and it'll be done."

"All right, sir," Mark said. "If I see with my own eyes that you become invisible, you can lead the charge."

Silence reigned, all eyes on Reese. Theron glanced at each man, seeing the disbelief. Magic potions were for magic shows, not black ops rescues.

Reese turned off the burner, and picked up the flask with a potholder he'd retrieved from the bag. He swirled the cloudy liquid for half a minute then touched the side of the glass and swirled again. He lifted it up and stared into the flask. "Here goes."

Reese gulped down the contents and shivered. "Uh. Just as bad as I remember." He set the flask in the back of the car and picked up the Bunsen burner and did the same.

For a moment, Theron could see through Reese, into the car. And then he was gone.

Zack's eyes widened. "Whoa! I don't believe it."

"No way!" Trey said.

Surprisingly, Mark took it in stride. "Reese, I guess you're leading the charge. Kathleen." She turned to him as he pulled a paper out of his pocket and handed it to her. " Here's the number I want you to call fifteen minutes after we go inside. Tell him exactly what's written there."

Kathleen took the note, read through it, and slipped it into her pocket. "You can count on me."

Mark scanned the group with a frown. "Reese? I'll give you two minutes from the time you open the door before the rest of us swarm in."

"Got it."

Theron hadn't realized that Reese had moved until he heard his voice beside Kathleen.

Mark checked his watch then headed to his SUV. "Let's move out."

They scrambled into the vehicles and Jason drove down the road behind Mark's car, following him into a corner of the parking lot, and parked beside him.

Jason turned to Kathleen. "Mom, once we're out of the

car, I want you to put a bubble around it."

She squeezed his arm. She acted tough, but Theron could see the tension in her shoulders and tightness around her eyes. "I will. Don't worry about me. You go in there and rescue your sister."

Jason turned farther around. "Go, Dad. Be careful. We'll be right behind you."

The back door opened and closed. It was a bit creepy. Theron kept his eyes on the front door of the building. He couldn't track Reese, so it was the only place to look to know his progress.

The door opened and Jason checked his watch and mumbled. "Two minutes."

Kathleen reached behind the seat and grabbed Theron's hand and put the other on Jason's arm. "Be careful. Bring my baby back to us." Unshed tears clouded her eyes.

Theron squeezed her hand. "We will." Nothing would stop him from getting to Jamie now.

The doors on the other SUV opened. Yes! Theron got out as Jason did. It was obvious that Jason and the three other guys were a team. They moved as a unit and Theron followed behind. As they neared the door, all four men ahead of him drew out guns. He didn't have one, but he'd relied on his martial arts skills to get him out of two risky situations. That would work just fine this time, too.

They stepped through the door and paused. A man sat frozen at the desk squarely in front of them, unblinking eyes not registering them. Theron hadn't expected the catatonic potion to make people appear to be statues.

Zak hurried behind the desk, and lowered the man to the floor. He zip tied the man's hands and feet, and pushed him under the desk.

Mark spoke in a harsh whisper. "Let's move out."

A hallway stretched left and right, the floor covered in

gray commercial carpet. That should quiet their footsteps.

The three men stealthily headed right.

Theron stayed behind Jason as he peeked into and crept past three offices at the front of the building. At the first corner, Jason peeped around it then continued down the hall. He checked each room as they passed, weaving from one side of the hall to the other. At the third door, he pulled back and held up two fingers, pointing left and to himself.

Theron followed behind as Jason ran in and yanked one man from a chair before either man realized they were there. Both had been reading as they sat at a table. He fleetingly wondered if this was the room Kathleen had seen when she held the rabbit's foot.

The other man was halfway out of his chair when Theron reached him. The guy was taller than Theron, but not as muscular. A punch sent the man sprawling back into his chair. Theron threw him to the floor, face first, and yanked his arms behind him. He slid a zip tie around the guy's wrists, fumbled with threading it, then pulled it tight.

Jason tied Theron's man's ankles, as Theron punched the guy in the side of the head, knocking him out.

Back in the corridor, Jason checked more rooms. At the last one, he held up one finger. Theron followed him into the room. Bunk beds sat against the right and left walls. One man slept in the lower left bunk. Jason tiptoed up, punched him in the side of the head, pulled back the blankets and tied the man's wrists and ankles then pulled the covers back up.

Theron shook his head at how the guy would react when he woke.

At the corner of the corridor, Jason lifted one finger.

Theron peeked, seeing a man with a holstered gun standing beside a door. That had to be the basement. "Let me get this one." He stepped out, punched the air, sending a wave of energy towards the man, and the man flew back about five feet.

Jason clapped him on the back, and whispered. "You tie him up. I'll check the rest of these rooms."

Theron raced down the hall as the man shook his head and leaned forward. He thrust at the air again, pushing the man to his back. Theron stopped beside him, struck his face to knock him out, then zip tied him. Faster than the last time. He checked the nearest room to make sure it was empty, then dragged the man inside.

He stepped into the hallway as Jason returned.

Jason reached the door first. "All clear. Let's head down." He grabbed the knob. "Damn. It's locked."

Theron turned back. "I'll check the guard's pockets." He found a set of keys in the right pants pocket and returned to the door, handing the keys to Jason.

The third key worked.

At the bottom of the stairs, they stopped at a door. Jason put his hand on the doorknob. "You did so well with the other guard, you might as well go first this time."

Theron nodded and stepped through the doorway. A man sat beside a door, reading a book. He glanced up as the door opened, and jumped to his feet, dropping his book on the floor. Theron punched the air and the man flew, sliding along the wall. His head hit the far side of the next door frame, knocking him out.

Jason rushed past Theron, checked the guard's pockets and tossed keys to Theron. "Go get Jamie."

A door down the hall slammed open, and four men strut single file into the corridor. Jason stood as Theron pocketed the keys. Jason hadn't gotten the chance to zip tie the guy on the floor.

"Looks like we've got a security breach," the largest of the men said.

Two pulled guns at the same time Jason did. This might

not end well.

Theron whipped up his arms, thrusting with both fists, knowing he had to put extra energy into the push to hit two with enough force. One gunman fell back against the doorframe and grunted, his gun falling from his hand and skittering across the floor. The second gunman bumped against another man, but both kept their balance.

Jason took advantage of the disruption and launched himself at the second gunman while the gun was facing away from them. They went down and Jason punched the guy's face.

Theron rushed in and physically kicked the third guy, a redhead, as he sent his force into the fourth. Neither man went down. He'd have to think of this as if he was sparring with Eric and keep the man between him and the other one.

The empty-handed gunman came up behind Jason and Theron pushed some force at him so that he overshot and landed on his knees.

The redhead roared and came at Theron. He wasn't as disciplined as the fighters Theron was used to, and Theron easily put him into a chokehold. That left Theron open for attack by the fourth man, who punched the side of his head. Theron released his hold with one hand and thrust energy at the man beside him, pushing him into the wall.

Theron tightened his hold on the redhead until the man sagged. He dropped him, hoping the man was unconscious and not pretending. The fourth man took two running steps towards Theron when Theron sidestepped, grabbed the man's arm and pushed him, adding to his momentum as his head struck the wall. He slid to the floor.

Theron glanced at Jason, who seemed in control of his men. Theron zip tied both men and headed down the corridor, concentrating on catching his breath.

He pulled the keys from his pocket and stopped in front

of the door beside the chair. He'd spent weeks trying to get to Jamie, and now he was about to succeed. His hands trembled as he tried the keys, the fourth opening the door. He took one step inside to survey the room.

"Theron!"

He snapped his head toward Jamie's voice. He hadn't heard it in so long, he almost thought he'd imagined it.

A man who looked vaguely familiar stood sideways, holding her against his chest.

Jamie held up her hand. "Hold on, Theron. Adam, it's okay."

She didn't seem distressed, so he stayed in the doorway and drank her in. Her dark, wavy hair glowed under the fluorescent lights. She might be a bit thinner than last he'd seen her, but that wasn't a surprise.

"This is my boyfriend, Theron. He's here to rescue us."

Adam pulled Jamie tighter against him. "Jamie, don't go with him. I'll take you anywhere you want to go. I'll protect you. I won't let Dad do anything to your baby."

Jamie was pregnant!

Jamie struggled enough to turn and face Adam. "Dad?" She screeched. "Connor is your father? The man who forced me to kill people? The man who tried to kill my baby, is your father?"

Theron felt like he'd been gut punched at the thought that their baby might have been killed. He flew across the room and yanked Adam's arm behind his back, lifting it higher, until Adam released Jamie.

Adam struggled against Theron's hold. "Jamie, I didn't know he was going to kidnap you. He was ecstatic when we went on our first date, but you wouldn't go out with me again after the second. He had me take a class with you every semester, even after I graduated, in hopes that you'd go out with me again."

"You purposely had classes with me? Why?" She stood in front of Adam with her hands on her hips.

Jamie had never mentioned Adam to him. She must not have considered him important. He did sort of remember seeing him talk to Jamie occasionally. He wanted to slam Adam to the floor, but he might have important information.

"When you were born, our fathers arranged a betrothal between us. We were supposed to spend summers together and eventually get married. But your adopted parents killed your real parents, and ruined their plans."

A grunt from the doorway caught his attention. Jason's face showed anger, but not surprise. Was it true?

Jamie curled her fingers and hit Adam in the jaw with the heel of her hand. His face contorted and he groaned.

"No! My parents aren't murderers. They wouldn't have killed my birth parents."

Theron pushed him to the floor, and braced a foot on his back.

Adam whined. "Jamie, I love you. We're supposed to be together."

Jamie kicked Adam in the ribs, not as hard as he would have. "No way, Adam." She threw herself at Theron.

He buried his face in her hair. It had been so long since he'd smelled her unique scent. He swung her up into his arms and she squealed. "Theron, I can walk."

"I don't want to let you go yet." He glanced at Jason. "Tie him up."

He strode out of the room and to the door for the stairs.

She tightened her grip on his neck. "Wait!"

Theron stopped. "What's the matter?"

"I need to tell you something before we join everybody."

He kissed her. "About the baby? I think it's wonderful that you're having our baby."

She relaxed a bit, and stared at her knees. "To save our

baby's life, I had to do something I vowed never to do."

He tightened his hold on her. He sensed this was the thing she'd held back before. Some ability she was ashamed or afraid of. "Baby, whatever it is, you did it for a good reason."

"I know, but…" She hid her head in his neck, then pulled away. "Connor found out I was pregnant. Now I know he wanted me to have Adam's baby, so this one was in his way. He had me tied up and a doctor came to do an abortion. I…compelled them to believe they'd actually done it."

Theron turned at the strangled noise behind him.

Jamie stiffened and tightened her hold on him. "Jason, that was only the second time I've used it and the first time was an accident."

Theron didn't understand the tension. Yes, it was an ability that could more often than not be used to do evil things, but Jamie wouldn't do that.

Tears ran down Jamie's cheeks, her eyes still on Jason. "I never told you I could do it because of how much you hated that Nathan used it to hurt all those people. I didn't want you to hate me."

Theron glared at Jason. "Jamie did the only thing she could to save your niece or nephew. What about you, Jason? You've killed to save lives. Is this worse?"

Jason sucked in a breath. The seconds ticked by. "No, it's not." He swept past them and pulled the door open, waiting for them to go through. He didn't look at his sister. He preceded them up the stairs and held that door, too.

As they approached the last turn in the corridor, Theron heard many voices. They came into the entry area, full of uniformed police.

Jason glanced back. "Come talk to Mark."

"Theron, you can put me down now," Jamie whispered.

"Not until we're in front of your mother." He stopped next to Mark.

168

Mark grinned. "Good. You found her. Hi, Jamie. Do you need medical attention?"

"No. I'm fine. Theron just doesn't want to let me go."

Mark chuckled. "Why don't you join your parents? I'll send a detective over shortly."

"Thanks, Mark," Theron said. "We couldn't have rescued Jamie without you."

Mark clapped him on the shoulder. "Hey. I couldn't let anything happen to Jason's little sister."

Theron strode through the open doors to the corner of the parking lot.

Kathleen jumped out of the car and raced the last few steps toward them. "Jamie, are you hurt?"

"No, Mom. Theron won't put me down."

Theron lowered her legs and let her slide down his body.

She hugged her mother. "Are Abby and Shauna okay?"

"They're fine." Kathleen pulled back and studied her daughter's face. "I'm so glad to have you back." She squinted. "You're pregnant."

Jamie's eyes widened. "Mom, how can you know that?"

"When I hugged you, I sensed the little life."

Theron wrapped an arm around Jamie's waist. He hoped he silently communicated to Kathleen that he would stand by Jamie.

Kathleen nodded, studied him. "That's how you could sense Jamie. Your blood runs through the baby and connects you to her."

Disappointment swamped him. "You mean I won't feel this connection after the baby is born?"

"That's my guess, but I don't know for sure. Reese didn't have a connection with our children."

Her eyes riveted on something behind him, so he glanced over his shoulder. Jason approached.

Jason stopped beside Jamie and Kathleen took his hand.

"Did you see your dad?"

He frowned and shook his head.

"It's been over an hour. He's likely blind by now and doesn't want to distract anyone to ask for help."

He squeezed his mother's hand. "I'll go bring him out." He turned and jogged back into the building.

Kathleen's expression blanked for several seconds, then she smiled.

Jamie grabbed her mother's arm. "What do you mean, he's blind? And what's he doing in there if he's blind?"

Kathleen hugged her daughter. "Jamie, it's all right. It's a short-term side effect of the potion he took to help you."

Jamie glared at the building. "He could have been hurt! There are bad guys with guns in there."

"I just talked to him and he's fine."

Jamie's legs buckled, and Theron took her to the car and opened the door.

She rubbed her arms. "I can't get in there yet. I haven't been outdoors in weeks."

"It's all right." He leaned back against the car and pulled her against him, wrapping his arms around her. She leaned her head back against his chest. It was wonderful holding her again. He kissed the top of her head. She covered his arms with hers.

A few minutes later, he spotted Jason with Reese in tow. The older man had hold of Jason's elbow and their pace was slower than normal. A uniformed officer kept in step beside Jason as they talked.

They neared and Kathleen threw herself at her husband. "Reese, you made it."

His arms circled her. "Of course, I did. Where's Jamie?"

"Right here, Dad." She wrapped her arms around his waist and hugged him. "I'm fine. Thanks for helping rescue me."

He kissed the top of her head. "I'd do anything for my little girl."

Theron's heart constricted at the love these two people had for their child. It made him think of *his* child that he'd known about for all of twenty minutes, and how much he loved it already.

Kathleen led Reese to the car and he leaned against it.

Jason wrapped his arms around his sister, and whispered. "I'm so glad we found you. I love you, Jamie." At least, that was a halfway apology for the way he'd reacted to Jamie's story.

Jason stepped back. "Jamie, this is Officer Davidson. He has questions for you."

As Davidson led her through the questions, Theron felt her stiffen occasionally. It had to be difficult to give as much information as possible to make sure that Connor was arrested, but not give away anyone's abilities.

He had the hardest time when Jamie explained how Connor had played with her, telling her she could escape if she successfully fought through the men he set up. She told the officer how Theron had taught her to fight and she reached the door, but it was locked. He worried that she'd tell the officer she had killed some of them, but she told him that since the men failed at preventing her from reaching the door, Connor had them all killed. It was the truth, that Connor was the reason they died. At least it solved another case for Davidson.

Theron listened to a sanitized picture of what Jamie had gone through, but he was sure there was so much more that she couldn't reveal to an outsider.

One thing that irked him was that Jamie didn't implicate Adam. She said he'd been imprisoned with her. He sensed nothing had happened between them, but wondered how close they'd gotten. She'd spent four weeks in the same room with the man, but had kicked him when she'd left.

After Davidson finished his questioning, Jamie sagged against him.

He pushed away from the car and opened the door. "Let's sit inside."

She scrambled in and he sat beside her. She snuggled into him and soon fell asleep. Theron rubbed her back. He couldn't keep his hands off her. Every second, he needed to make sure she was all right. He kissed the top of her head, and swore to do his best to make sure nothing like this ever happened to her again.

He closed his eyes and leaned his head back, feeling at peace for the first time in weeks.

Chapter 18

Jamie woke with Adam's arm wrapped around her, bare chest plastered to bare chest. In a split second, her heart and lungs went from sleepy relaxed to racing as if she were a gazelle running from a lion. She'd tried so hard to keep distance between them, and now there was no separation. A hand rubbed her arm.

"No!" She shoved against a hard chest and pushed.

"Shh-shh. Jamie, you're safe."

"Theron." She sagged onto him. Panic attack averted.

Sunlight peeked in around the drapes in the large window beside the motel room door. Gray shadows filled the room. For weeks, there'd been only bright light or no light, except for a bit creeping at the edge of the bathroom door they would leave ajar.

She tipped her head up and buried her nose in his neck. She should have noticed Theron's scent when she woke. How could it both calm and excite her?

They'd had to stay the night. She'd wanted to go directly home once they left Connor's compound, but Jason had things to wrap up and the police needed her to stick around longer. Something about having more questions for her after questioning all the suspects. Mark had convinced the police to let her go after one more interview in the morning. And

Theron thought she'd travel better after a good night's sleep.

She'd persuaded her parents to go home as soon as they'd gotten to the motel, and talked her dad into letting her mom drive. She was afraid that there would be aftereffects of being blind.

Tears leaped to her eyes at the lengths her family took to rescue her. Her mom's exhaustion from trying to reach Jamie's mind, and touching dead bodies to read their history. Her dad using a spell he knew would blind him. And Jason and Theron coming into a building protected by armed men with who knew what abilities.

She'd almost pushed Theron away. "I'm sorry."

He gave her a quick squeeze. "Nothing to be sorry about, baby. You've been through a lot."

"It's just that, I spent the last month sleeping in a bed with another man." Theron stiffened beneath her, but she plowed on. He must have noticed only one bed. "And I kept a pillow between us, but sometimes when I woke, his arm would be over me with the pillow squished to my back. And just now, for a second, I thought—"

"Shh." Theron levered up with her still in his arms and snuggled her into his lap. He kissed the underside of her jaw. "It's over. And he's not ever coming near you again." He gently placed a hand on each side of her face.

She dragged her eyes up to his warm brown ones.

His lips touched hers, just barely, and he pulled back. "I love you."

She blinked away tears. "I know. It's what got me through. Knowing you love me and wouldn't stop looking for me." She kissed him. "Sometimes I imagined directing my love to you. Hoping it reached you, so you'd know I was still alive." She burrowed her face into his neck, dragging the scent of Theron into her lungs, into her soul.

His hug surrounded her in love. "I felt it. I still went a

little crazy, but feeling you were alive gave me hope."

She kissed his neck, soft and warm. Her lips tingled as she planted little kisses in a trail to his lips. "Theron, make love to me."

She'd been exhausted when they went to bed the night before. Theron had stripped them both, and slipped into bed beside her. He'd tucked her close to him, and that's what she needed most. Now, she needed more, his kisses, his touch, for him to be inside her.

He lay back and rolled them to their sides, so they faced each other. "I've had way too many dreams about this." He kissed her. Oh, what a kiss. Any before it was a prelude to the love he poured into this one.

She felt all his pent up worry and longing. His strength and compassion. They'd barely gotten to know each other's bodies before she'd been snatched away. She ran a hand over his muscular chest that seemed bigger than she remembered.

He made love to her in the sweetest way.

***

Jamie dozed on and off on the way home, snuggled into Theron's side, the most relaxed she'd been in weeks. Freedom also meant windows. Every time she woke, besides staring at Theron, her eyes were glued to the passing scenery. Cars and trucks, sunshine and trees, people and life. And when she asked, Jason pulled over for her to get out of the car. She was no longer trapped.

They passed the Rawlins town limits sign. "Jason, I think Theron and I should go to Mom and Dad's, so you newlyweds can have your house to yourselves. Now that the danger's over."

His eyes met hers in the rearview mirror. "You don't have to."

"I know. But you had to put up with this guy for too long." She nudged Theron. "Thanks for everything."

Theron's arm tightened around her. "Yeah, thanks, Jason."

"No thanks needed. I'd do anything for my little sister."

Jamie glanced down a side street. "Um, Jason. Mom and Dad's is that way."

Jason glanced back. "I know, but you might as well collect the rest of your stuff. And I need to talk to you."

Jamie didn't like the sound of that. They'd had breakfast to talk. They'd had more than two hours in the car to talk. This must require a face-to-face with no eavesdroppers. And it scared her.

Theron squeezed her hand. "Jason, can't it wait until tomorrow? Jamie's exhausted."

She would have been fine, except the police interrogation had taken two hours. They probably knew she held back information. Beforehand, Jason had taken her through the questions they might ask. She had kept as close to the truth as she could, but with repeated questions, worded in different ways, she may have slipped up and contradicted herself.

His main concern was that someone would connect the burns on the two men's necks to her. He wasn't worried that she'd killed them. He assured her it was self defense. He didn't want the circus that would ensue if her heating ability was discovered.

"Sorry, Jamie. But I think it's better to cover this before you go back to Mom and Dad's."

Theron expelled a breath and kissed her temple. "I'm right beside you."

Jason was driving. Again, she didn't have a choice.

Jason turned into his driveway and they got out. He and Theron retrieved their bags from the back and they went inside.

Jason dropped his bag beside the door. "Shauna, I'm home!"

Jamie smiled at the squeal from somewhere in the house.

Shauna raced down the stairs. "Jamie!" She hugged her sister-in-law. "I'm so glad you're safe."

They'd had such a short time to get to know each other, but Jamie felt the love of a sister in the hug. "I am, too. And I'm *never* doing that again."

Then Shauna launched herself at Jason. He staggered a bit and laughed. "I was only gone four days and I talked to you every night."

"I know. But I missed you and you were fighting bad guys."

"I missed you, too." He kissed her.

"Shauna." Something had wiped away Jason's light mood.

Jamie tensed.

"Jamie and Theron are going to stay at Mom and Dad's. Can you gather their stuff while I talk to Jamie about the Ghost of Christmas Past?"

That was some code. Jamie had no idea what he meant, but Shauna turned pasty. "You don't want me—"

He took her hand. "I'm okay with it now."

A chill slithered up Jamie's spine. It had to be bad if Jason needed to work through whatever it was. "Um, can we get it over with because this is scaring me. I have a feeling I don't want to hear it."

Jason sighed. "You don't, but you need to. Let's go into the living room."

Jamie sat in the middle of the couch with Theron beside her, holding her hand. Jason pushed the coffee table out a bit and lowered himself to it in front of her. She wasn't liking this. At. All.

"I'll start with the dreams Hannah gave me."

"Mom's Hannah? Why would—"

"Who's Hannah?" Theron asked.

Jamie glanced at him. "She's an ancestor of Mom's. She came to Mom in dreams when she first got to Rawlins and taught her how to use her abilities." She turned back to Jason. "So, why did *Mom's* ancestor come to *you*?"

That was a reminder that Jamie and Jason had been adopted. There couldn't have been more love between all of them if they'd been blood.

"Because...I'll get to that." Jason sat taller. "Hannah showed me how I would have turned out if our birth parents had lived. And I hated that me. In the vision, I told a girl that I was bringing her to dinner at my parents' house. We walked into that mansion and I introduced her to Nathan. And dragged her to the basement."

Jamie couldn't take the pain in Jason's eyes. She took his hand. "Jason, you don't have to say more. I know where this is going."

"Jamie, if not for Mom and Dad. I'd be a killer." His voice broke on the last word.

She dropped to her knees in front of her brother. "No. You wouldn't. You couldn't."

He hugged her. "We would have been raised to enjoy hurting people. Killing and wanting more. Sacrificing for more power."

She pulled back. "But it was just a dream."

He shook his head. "No. It's likely what would have been. All along the Proctor line, each parent trained his children to be just like him." He dropped his hands on her shoulders. "That would have been us."

She couldn't imagine anything worse than the vision of a Jason in another time enjoying killing a woman.

He took a deep breath and let it out slowly. "Sit back down. There's more."

The blood of evil men and women ran through them. And their birth father probably wasn't the worst. Jason likely was right. If they'd been raised by that man, they would have been as evil as him. She could see how it would have happened. Over the last few weeks, she'd been boxed into corners, forced to do what she never would have thought possible. If she'd been trained from a young child, she wouldn't have learned right from wrong. It would have been easy to do all those things, and worse. She shuddered.

Theron cupped her face in his hands, his warm, brown eyes shining with love, and filling her. "Jamie, that's not who you are. You were loved and raised by good people to become the real you."

She had to believe that was true. She kissed the palm of his hand then pulled it down to her lap.

She better understood why she'd been taken. If she'd had that other life, she would already be married to Adam, creating evil children with him. Except Adam wasn't evil. He'd been a friend and treated her with care. He must have known Connor wanted them to have children together, and he could have raped her, but he hadn't even tried to seduce her. Maybe, with those other parents, she would have been the one corrupting Adam, changing him in a way his father hadn't been able to.

It was amazing what a difference parents made. She'd never thought about it like this before. Sure, she loved Kathleen and Reese, and knew they loved her and had given her a good life, but she'd never thought about how they'd replaced whatever evil she might have harbored with love.

She turned back to Jason. She didn't want to hear more, but steeled herself for worse, glad Theron was beside her. He believed in her goodness.

Shauna came in, set two bags beside the table and sat beside Jason. He wrapped an arm around her and touched his forehead to the side of her head.

After a few seconds, Jason took a deep breath and straightened. "Hannah also showed me the night Nathan and Elyse died. Only this time, Dad—Reese—got there too late." The pain in his voice was reflected in his eyes.

Jamie's heart pounded. She didn't know why this scared her more. "What? Too late for what?"

Jason's eyes glazed over, probably seeing that alternate time. "Mom was tied to the sacrificial table. Nathan plunged a knife into her heart just as Dad got there. Power swirled to Nathan and the others around the table. Then Nathan laughed and propelled the knife at Dad, killing him."

Jamie trembled. She didn't know how, but she knew that was almost what happened. Her loving parents came close to dying, almost leaving Jason and her in the hands of monsters.

Jason blinked. "What really happened is Dad got there just a bit sooner and rescued Mom from under the knife. Mom put all of those people into a bubble and threw fireballs into it."

Jamie covered her mouth. She understood how her mother would have felt taking those lives, doing it because there was no other choice. She sucked in a breath. "And Mom's had to live with that secret. I'm so glad she has Dad."

A month ago, she might have had a hard time believing her mother was capable of taking those lives, but no more. She had regrets about taking two lives, and wished she hadn't been forced into the situation, but knew if she had it to do over again, she'd likely do the same thing.

Jason shook his head, taking her hand. "I love you, Jamie. I wish I'd responded like that when I found out. Unfortunately, I had trouble dealing with it and left after Mom told me. That's when Hannah showed me what could have been."

"So, why did you tell me now?" Jamie asked.

"After Adam told you, I figured I'd better give you the details."

She frowned. "What did…Oh! I thought it was so unbelievable that I forgot."

He gave her a sad smile. "That's our Jamie. Only believing the best." He clasped her hand. "One more thing. I want to apologize for being angry with you when you said you'd compelled the doctor."

"Jason, I understand why you reacted like that. It's okay."

"No, it's not. Listen. The first thing that came to mind was how Nathan had compelled all those girls to do what he wanted. I'm sorry I made such a comparison. You're nothing like him."

Jason had an ability to know if a person was a virgin. It only had an evil purpose, so she did understand his hatred for those types of abilities. She covered her stomach. She hoped her baby didn't inherit an ability that had only an evil use.

"I accept your apology."

Shauna slid forward, taking Jamie's hand. "Doctor? Jamie, were you sick?"

Jamie slanted a glance at Jason before looking back at Shauna. "I'm surprised Jason didn't tell you. I'm pregnant."

Shauna lost her balance leaning forward to hug Jamie. Her husband steadied her. "Congratulations." She stood and grinned. "I'm going to be an aunt."

Jason stood and stepped away to allow Jamie and Theron to stand.

Theron held out his hand to Jason. "Thanks for everything."

"Like I said, I'd do anything to protect my little sister." He hugged Jamie.

She tightened her arms around him. He'd been there for her through so much. They'd had crazy things to deal with that other kids didn't.

Theron put his arm on her waist. "I'd rather not have Jamie drive separately. Do you mind if her car stays here for another day or so?"

"Not a problem. Why don't you leave her keys? We'll drive it over when we come for the family dinner." His eyes crinkled at her. "Because you know there's going to be one."

Jamie fished in her purse and handed the keys over. "Oh, yes."

At the door, Jamie turned back, but decided not to say anything more when she saw Jason whisper in Shauna's ear, causing her to blush. Jamie didn't want to think about what he had said.

She closed the door and took Theron's hand.

Chapter 19

Jamie rushed into the house and straight to the library. Her parents sat together on the couch and looked up in surprise.

"Jamie, you're back." Her mother's smile brightened her eyes.

Jamie pounced on the couch beside her mother, leaned across and hugged her, then included her father in the hug. "Mom, I love you. You, too, Dad. Thank you for saving Jason and me. I can't imagine how horrible we would have been without you."

Kathleen pushed her back and frowned. "Honey, what's this about?"

Jamie sat back on her lower legs. "Jason told me how...Nathan almost killed both of you...and you...took care of him, so he couldn't hurt anybody again." She hugged them again. "Thank you for loving us."

Reese gave her an extra squeeze. "We'll always love you."

She sat back. "Jason and I weren't loved by the Proctors. We were only tools to them. Not allowed to make our own choices."

Theron hovered in the doorway, his thumbs in his belt loops, a smile tugging his lips. She held out her hand to him.

"But I made a better choice."

He crossed the room, took her hand and, kissed the top of her head, then stared into her eyes.

If her parents weren't right beside her, she could get lost in those happy eyes.

"I made my choice, too." His voice was low, said just for her. One corner of his mouth tipped up. "But I didn't expect to start our family quite this soon."

"What?" It wasn't often her dad used that tone.

Yeah, not a happy Dad anymore.

Theron's thumb rubbed circles on her shoulder, a nice reminder that he was right there with her.

Jamie's eyes darted to her mother and back to her dad. "Mom didn't tell you?"

Kathleen shook her head. "I thought you should be the one to tell him."

Jamie rolled her eyes. "Thanks, Mom."

Jamie glanced at Theron. "Theron found out yesterday. I've known a few days, so it's still new to us." She bit her lip and gave her father a pleading stare.

Theron shifted a little. "And we're getting married. Soon. Definitely before the baby's born."

She twisted her head up. "We are?"

He smiled. Such a melting smile. "Jamie, I love you. Will you marry me?"

She giggled. She knelt on the couch, practically in her mother's lap, and he proposed as he towered over her.

"Yes!"

Theron lifted Jamie to the floor, turning her into his arms. He kissed her. On the mouth. In front of Mom and Dad. "That *wasn't* the way I'd planned to propose."

"You planned it? Even before you found out I was pregnant?"

"I planned it before I left school. That last time we were

supposed to meet up before you went home, was going to be my first attempt to get you to see me as more than a friend."

He looked over her shoulder at her parents, so she spun in his arms.

Her dad still looked like he was pulling himself together.

Reese stood. "I guess congratulations are in order." He held out his hand and Theron shook it.

"Thank you, sir. Jamie means the world to me."

***

Jamie stirred beside him, then lurched out of bed, grabbed her nightshirt and threw it over her head. She poked her arms out the sleeves by the time she reached the door.

Theron pulled on shorts and t-shirt and followed her out. She paused, facing the closed bathroom door, then raced into the bedroom next to it. He stopped in the doorway as she disappeared into the adjoining bathroom. He heard her throw up.

Abby got up from bed and stopped at the bathroom door. "Ew. Why are you throwing up in *my* bathroom?"

Jamie heaved again. "Tony was in the other one. Mom would kill me if I vomited in her hallway."

The toilet flushed and water ran in the sink.

Abby stepped into the bathroom. "Are you going to give me the flu?"

"No."

"Then why are you...Oh! Did they do this to you?" Her voice squeaked with panic.

Theron stepped into the room. "No, she got pregnant before."

Abby squealed and spun around. "Who are you?"

Abby had been unconscious when Jamie was kidnapped, and her parents had taken her away before she'd recovered.

The night before, Abby hadn't come home from her friend's house until after Jamie and he had gone to bed, so they hadn't met yet.

"Theron Jarvis. Jamie's…fiancé."

"You better be."

He chuckled.

"Hey, wait a minute. I thought you were Jamie's best friend."

"Haven't you heard? Best friends make the best husbands." He squeezed past Abby and put his arm around Jamie. "Feeling better?"

Jamie sighed. "Yeah. Let's go back to bed."

Abby's eyes widened. "Together?"

Theron grinned. "It's a little late for that, don't you think?"

Abby's face turned red.

"I'm going to enjoy having you for a little sister."

"I'm not little," she yelled at their backs.

Theron closed Jamie's bedroom door and trapped her against it. "Now, what did you have in mind?"

She ducked under his arm. "Talking." She got into bed.

He knew what they could do after talking, and started to push his shorts down.

"No. Leave those on. Everybody's up. I just want you to hold me while we talk."

That he could do. He hadn't held her enough since he got her back. He climbed into bed and pulled her close. Not quite as good as making love, but it would do. He leaned back so he could see her face. "Now, what do you want to talk about?"

"Are you going back to Boston for that job, now that I'm safe?"

He kissed her nose. "No. I'm not going to leave you. And I had planned to transfer to Amherst, but I think I need to get a job instead."

"No. You have to finish. It's just one more year."

"Well, I'm not going to be dependent on your parents. I can still finish. It'll just take a little longer."

She scraped a fingernail up and down on his chest. "Would you mind being dependent on me?"

"You're not going to work so I can go to school." He slid his hand between them and rested it on her stomach. "Besides, halfway through the school year, we're going to have a baby."

"I want to buy a house with my inheritance like Jason did."

There was only one source for the money he could think of, and he didn't like it. "What inheritance?"

He felt her stiffen. She wasn't comfortable talking about it, but she still planned to use the money.

"From the Proctors."

"You'd take money from the evil people who arranged your marriage when you were born?"

She pulled in a breath and let it out. "I knew they were murderers. Jason and I talked about the money a long time ago. I even drew up a chart with pluses and minuses. We first decided to accept or reject the money together."

"How old were you when you did that?"

"Mom and Dad told us about it when I was sixteen."

He shook his head. "I can't imagine making a decision like that when I was sixteen. What was the deciding factor, besides getting lots of money?" He grinned.

Her expression became somber. She gazed at him. "If we refused the inheritance, when Jason turned twenty-five it would go to another branch of the Proctor family. Jason researched them, and they aren't good people. We were afraid of what they'd do with the money."

He wondered if that branch of the Proctors had tried to

become guardians to Jamie and Jason to control the money. He could see them pleading for a generous allowance to take care of the children, and using all the money by the time Jamie and Jason became adults. Or worse, being abandoned when the money ran out early.

He hugged her, glad that his Jamie had been so well loved all her life.

He pulled back. "All right. We'll buy a house and you can support me for the school year." He dropped his brows. "But we don't go overboard."

Her eyes practically glowed. "And after you get a teaching job, the money becomes an emergency fund."

"Okay."

She grinned. "Thank you." She gave him a kiss and sat up.

He circled her waist. "Hey, where are you going? We're not finished talking."

She arched an eyebrow. "Talking?"

"Yes. Talking." He almost laughed. "Really."

She snuggled back under the covers. "Okay. Talk."

"When do you want to get married?"

"I don't know."

"I've heard that the bigger the wedding, the longer it takes."

She grinned. "I guess it's good that I don't want a big wedding. Just family and a few friends. Jason and Shauna's wedding in the library was nice."

"You wouldn't mind a small wedding? We could have it in a couple of weeks. I can drive back and get my mom." He'd totally forgotten about her. "I wonder if I should tell her about the baby before or after the wedding."

"Before. Otherwise, one of my family is likely to mention it to her at the wedding."

He nodded. "Good point. I'll call her today. Tell her

you've been rescued, and she's going to be a grandma, and to mark off her calendar for our wedding. That should cover it."

"One more thing." She grinned. "I love you and I'm so glad we're more than friends now."

He'd be thankful for that for the rest of his life. He kissed her. "I love you, too."

THE END

Adam's Redemption – Rawlins Book 4

A premonition has never been so important...

After months of therapy, Adam has recovered from his lifelong obsession with Jamie. He's ready to start a fresh life, but he has a premonition of a woman who will die at his brother's hands if he doesn't find and rescue her.

Trill awakens from a spell induced haze to find herself five months pregnant, with a stranger trying to convince her she needs to run from her home or die. She peeks into his terror filled vision, packs a bag and runs with him. But it isn't long before Adam's brother tracks them down and they have to run again.

Trill and Adam must use every bit of their abilities and spells to stay ahead of his brother. But he has too many tricks and they can't run forever. Is their love destined to die with her?

Books by Deborah Wallace

Rawlins Series (Paranormal Romance)
Kathleen's Legacy
Jason's Forbidden Woman
Jamie's Trials
Adam's Redemption
Kristy's Puzzle
Tony's to Protect – *Fall 2020*

Wounded Warrior Hearts Series
Wounded Warrior Hearts: Steven
Wounded Warrior Hearts: Amy
Wounded Warrior Hearts: Russ

Choice Series (Romantic Suspense)
Second Choice
Third Choice
No Choice
Her Choice
Series complete

Unknown Series (Romantic Suspense)
Father Unknown
Killer Unknown — *Summer 2002*

Other Books (Romantic Suspense)
I Shot the Sheriff
Your Love Belongs to Me
Summer Love
New Memories

Check out my website for details on these books and where to find them. You can also sign up to receive emails when I have a new book. www.DeborahWallaceBooks.com.

You can find my books on my Amazon author page. amazon.com/author/deborahwallacebooks

Thanks for reading. While you're waiting on the next story, if you would be so kind as to leave a review for this book, that would be wonderful. I appreciate the feedback and support. Reviews lift my spirits and boost my creativity. Thanks!

About Deborah Wallace

Deborah Wallace decided to try writing what she liked to read, and stories started populating her brain. Writing has become a passion, and she can't go long without touching her keyboard.

She's written in different genres, but the stories she keeps coming back to are her favorite, romantic suspense. The first *Rawlins* book was supposed to be the only paranormal. Then she asked 'what if...' and now children of the first characters and a couple of friends have books.

She wrote her first stories in 2014 but didn't publish until 2019.

She's been called a Jane-of-all-trades, from seamstress to house and furniture designer/builder to computer programmer to technical writer and bookkeeper. She even does car maintenance. All may help with details in a story.

Deborah grew up in Michigan, but Massachusetts has been her home for more years than she cares to think about. She loves the history, the museums and antique houses, the seacoast and hiking trails.

Now it's off to far flung places, at least in her mind.

www.ingramcontent.com/pod-product-compliance
Lightning Source LLC
Chambersburg PA
CBHW030331180626
46810CB00003B/1316